ROAR

TIM MARSHALL

ROAR

Published February, 2007

This novel is a work of fiction. Names, characters, places, and incidents either are the product of the author's imagination or are used fictitiously. Any resemblance to actual persons, living or dead, events or locales is entirely coincidental.

ISBN-13: 978-0-6151-4108-4

Printed in the United States of America

timtmarshall@msn.com

Thanks to my brothers, each of whom have contributed in some important way in making me and my life better. I am happier because you guys are around. Thank you to my father for teaching me to think. You are missed. And special thanks to the two women who have been, are, and always will be, the foundation under everything I do and accomplish - my mother, Karen and my wife, Lori. I am truly a lucky man.

- T.M.

"In an infinite and absolute random world, every possibility is a certainty."

— Forbes Maxwell

*   *   *   *   *

Tomorrow I am to be married to the most unlikely of women.

It is scheduled at 11:30 a.m. and is to be attended by nearly 400 guests, nearly all of whom are friends or relatives of hers. There have been 100 press passes issued for the reception.

I don't think I'm going to go.

If I did, the church would be embarrassingly out of balance. Only Marcus, my friend of many years, one of only three friends in my adult life, is planning to grace my side of the room and it's looking like he isn't going to make it. All that weight on one side would likely cause foundation problems and curvature of the spine. The church will look like it had a stroke.

*   *   *   *   *

Given a few more years, Dante no doubt would have been quite the lady's man. He was the talker. Jose was the more quiet of the two boys. On this day the two cousins were playing together as they often did, down the street from where they lived.

Technically, today they were further from home than they were supposed to be. Dante pointed out that since he'd turned twelve they should be able to go two blocks further than when he was only eleven like Jose. Jose wasn't sure about the logic but he figured if they got caught, he'd blame it on Dante.

Besides, they had more important things to think about.

"What do you think it is?" Jose asked.

"I have no clue. What do you think?"

They were looking at what appeared to be a perfectly round, black spot against a brick wall.

"It doesn't look real."

"I know. It's too… black." Dante said. "That can't be paint."

They had taken a short cut through the alley. The midday sun lit the alley surprisingly well. About 200 feet in, across from an overflowing dumpster, they came across the spot.

"Touch it." Dante suggested.

"You touch it."

3

Dante looked around and found an empty Mad Dog bottle. He picked it up and tossed it at the spot. Both boys cringed slightly in anticipation of the crash.

There was none.

"Whoa! Did you see that?" Dante said. "It just disappeared."

Jose picked up a piece of concrete and tossed it hard at the spot. It too disappeared.

"That's too weird. Its like it just absorbs stuff." Jose said.

The two boys spent the better part of the next twenty minutes throwing anything they could find at the spot. Always with the same result. Whatever they threw at it disappeared the second it made contact with the surface. Stuff didn't fade away. It went from being there to instantly not being there. Not even a sound.

The boys had run out of convenient ammunition.

"Touch it." Dante suggested once again.

"You touch it." Came the familiar response. But even as Jose was saying it, he was getting closer to the spot. Driven by curiosity, he moved within inches of the blackness.

"You're a chicken. You…" Dante said.

As Dante spoke, Jose reached out.

"Holy shit!" Jose said, jumping back.

"What? What did it feel like?"

"It felt weird. Very…weird." Jose said.

4

"Weird? Like what?"

"Like… nothing."

"Nothing?"

"Yeah. Try it."

Dante walked up to the spot and gingerly touched it, his fingertips instantly disappearing into the blackness.

"That is weird!" He said smiling. "Watch this." He stuck in his arm up to his elbow.

"Cool." Jose said. "Can you feel your arm at all?"

"I don't think so."

"Pull it back out."

Dante did.

"Can you feel it now?" Jose asked.

"Yeah. It feels fine." Dante massaged his arm just to be sure.

"Stick your head in." Jose said.

"Yeah right."

"Come on. Your arm's fine. Your head will be fine. And maybe you can see what's back there."

"I stuck my arm in. I'm the only one with any guts here." Dante taunted his younger cousin. "If you're so sure my head will be fine, stick yours in."

Jose knew he was right. He walked to within inches of the spot.

"I'm not afraid." He said, probably more to himself than to Dante.

He looked at the spot letting his fingers disappear and reappear back and forth across the plane of its surface. In his head he already knew what he was going to do. He wasn't going to stick his head in.

"Come on you pussy." Dante said.

"Yeah?" Jose was rocking back and forth from his heels to his toes. "Watch this."

And he jumped, completely disappearing into the spot.

"Cool! Jose! What do you see?"

No answer.

There was no answer for the next 15 minutes. 15 minutes which seemed like a lifetime. 15 turned to 30. Dante was supposed to be looking out for his cousin.

"Jose!" He called out for the hundredth time.

Finally, with no alternative, Dante inched closer to the spot. He had to help Jose. He couldn't let him disappear.

Dante felt tears.

And he too jumped into the blackness. And he too disappeared.

Neither boy was ever heard from again.

*   *   *   *   *

Now, in the spirit of honesty, the story you just read is fiction. The basic facts are true – the boys' names, the fact they disappeared, the existence of the "hole", etc. but the dialog, I just made it up. I wasn't there. No one was. I just thought it might be nice to start with a story. To kind of warm you up as a reader and warm me up as a writer.

What I do know as fact is this:

Orlando Sentinel – (Local News section, page B8) "Two Boys Missing – Two boys, Dante Garcia, age 12 and his cousin, Jose Murphy, age 11, were reported missing yesterday evening. According to the parents, both boys are "very independent" but did not say anything that gave any insight into their disappearance. A brief search was organized by the Orange County Sheriff's Department but was called off shortly after it began due to darkness. The search is scheduled to resume at daybreak."

Dante and Jose were the first to disappear. This was the first official mention I could find related to one of the important events I am about to share with you tonight. I've been doing some research lately to better relate this tale to you. I found this on microfilm in the Forbes Maxwell Memorial Library. As you will later see, I did know Forbes Maxwell but, as I mentioned, I never knew Dante or Jose. I didn't even know their names until just recently but I have chosen to think that they were good kids. In some cases, we *can* choose our delusions. I'll share with you shortly what happened to the boys, but for now, you'll have to be satisfied with this amazing coincidence - The aunt of the boys was the neighbor of my former landlady's sister.

Now, I know that it's not all that amazing but it was to my landlady. And coincidences are a big part about what this book is about.

*   *   *   *   *

A cavernous space, the human brain, abuzz with activity, like a Jetsons cartoon. Neurons exploding, spraying neurotransmitters with odd names like dopamine, across synapses to where they nestle, lock in key, into the next neuron and begin another whip of energy running down the beginning of another nerve resulting in yet another explosion. And so on. Chain reactions crack like whips, turning electricity into memories, urges, beliefs, philosophies, belches and grocery lists.

As the chemical carrier pigeons fly across synapses like George Jetson on his way to work, other chemicals, both natural and unnatural, try to way-lay the message - some attempting to ambush it and kill it off all together and others trying to stop the

8

chemicals that are out to stop the message. Such is the human mind.

Like nearly everything natural, it is beautiful. Like anything complicated, it breaks down. Like anything natural and complicated, it breaks down often but usually works anyway.

*   *   *   *   *

While my brain and its neurons have functioned within the realm of "normal" for most of my life, it's never been totally right, always with it's share of beeps and burps. Several evenings, particularly in college, after 1:00 a.m. on weekends, it shut down all together, leaving me with nothing but an empty memory, a hang-over and a pasty white substance in the corners of my mouth.

It has however, for the most part, served me well.

Would I know if it hadn't? Fair question. No one who has known me has ever seemed to think there was a problem but you always have to wonder. I'll continue along my reality, content with the knowledge that although my brain baggage is always in question - it's the only bag I have.

Some people, perhaps most, have a real problem with their baggage and in the end that is, I guess, what every story is about. This one is no different.

It's about my baggage and the misplaced baggage of my friend Marcus. It's about the designer bags of Mrs. Colleen Fisher, First Lady of the United States and the mismatched bags of Norman Hurst, one time lover of classical music and the holder of three patented earth moving inventions. It's about the lost baggage of Forbes Maxwell, who you shall meet shortly. It's about explanations and the unexplained. It's about the bags of authors and doctors and bartenders and fools.

Which brings us back to me.

Before my non-wedding, I'd like to unpack some of the bags I have.

*   *   *   *   *

Before you think ill of me for considering marooning my bride-to-be at the altar, let me tell you a little about myself. I am a 5' 8" balding, 58 year old white man. I lean toward Armani now but, at the beginning of this tale, I preferred plaid shorts although I did know enough to avoid wearing them with black socks. I was unemployed, poor, excessively average and living in a redecorated one room apartment above the garage of Mrs. Eugene Hayes, an 87 year old widow of 30 years who thought the $200 rent I paid her was a king's ransom. Who was I to squelch the illusions of an old woman?

Today, I am a reasonably clever, formerly overweight, ex-therapist who is scheduled to marry a woman whose beauty extends to the core of her soul.

I am also very, very wealthy, famous, and running a marathon would be a matter of "how fast" not "what if." I am a proud owner of one of the most expensive and ugly cars on earth and... I am very, very sorry for being the coward that I am.

Tomorrow I may feel different. That is often the case. But for tonight, I don't think I can do it. We'll see... we'll see.

*   *   *   *   *

My brain baggage is not particularly well organized but I like to think this is mostly by choice. I lose quite a bit because of this but oftentimes something long forgotten will drop out of a drawer in the backrooms of my mind, catch a ride on a breeze and blow in front of my consciousness.

For example, I just remembered something you may find interesting about one of my friends -   Forbes Maxwell owned exactly 5 ties, one for each day of the work week. Now he has become one of the most important religious writers since the Old Testament. Interestingly, he was also allergic to churches. Or more accurately, he was allergic to the dust mites which frequent old churches. Whenever he entered one, particularly an old,

11

cathedral sort of church, his eyes would water, his nose would run like someone had turned on a spigot and he fell into violent sneezing fits.

He shared this with me when we went out after my first day of work. It was the first and last time we went out together, not because we didn't like each other, we just didn't like to drink the same things or go to the same places. Forbes was one of those rare individuals who could disagree with you but make you feel good about it.

*   *   *   *   *

Years ago, when we were still working together in a smallish community mental health center called Seaview Behavioral Health Center, Forbes Maxwell finished writing another book in the "You're OK and I'm even OKer" vain. He'd published a couple of novels already and told me once that people would buy anything that reaffirmed what they already knew. The formula, developed by his agent to whom I will introduce you shortly, was written in yellow chalk on a black board in his office:

$$0c + 0k = \$$$

Translated it meant: "Ask for zero change and add zero new knowledge = Lots of books."

Forbes was an extremely intelligent but uncomplicated man who was well on his way to becoming a decent selling author. However, he was then, and remained until his untimely death, somewhat of an idiot savant.

The trick to selling self help books, he would say, was not to write anything that would cause people to think, because nobody really wanted to think anyway. To really sell books you needed to write something that people could buy thinking about change and then read and realize that they were already wonderful and didn't need to. It was a bonus if you could make them feel even better about themselves for taking the time to be so introspective to buy a book to try to change in the first place. At times, Forbes didn't make a whole lot of sense.

Forbes' agent was a woman by the name of Karen Eli Windslow and she met with him regularly to tell him how great an author he was and told him not to change a thing about his books. At that time, Karen Eli Windslow drove a Mercedes and lived alone in a four-bedroom house amid the upscale dwellings of Winter Park, Florida. Forbes Maxwell drove a 1991 Neon worth about $800 and lived alone in an apartment with an eat-in kitchen. As I am writing this, Karen owns three different homes, including a beach front mansion on the Gulf coast. Forbes is… well let me tell you a little more about the man before I share with you what happened to him.

Forbes had started his adult career as a mathematics teacher, which was an interesting choice since he didn't do well with kids. He was the kind of man who washed his hands both before and after he went to the bathroom and quickly became a prime target for the seemingly endless supply of verbal abuse that only teenagers can author. He quit teaching and decided to go into Social Work which was an equally inept career choice. In theory, Forbes loved people. Face to face with them however, he didn't fare so well. So while his books sold, he was unable to maintain a private practice and ended up at Seaview, a federally funded private, non profit community mental health center where the people he counseled had no choice but to sit across from him as he fumbled through his therapy.

Forbes had an office down and across the hall from me. There was a wall clock on the wall that didn't work because Forbes had removed the batteries. The ticking had made him nervous. He had a window, a perk upper management gave him after he published his first book.

"How you doing Thomas?" he asked each time I entered his office.

"I'm OK." I answered as scripted.

"Yes you are." He responded again as scripted. In all the time I'd worked with Forbes, he'd said this every time I had entered his office. And every time he said it, he'd sneak a glance at the dust free, hardbound editions of the books he'd written which were prominently displayed on the book shelf next to his desk. Please don't extrapolate from this that Forbes Maxwell was an egotistical man. He was far from it. It is just that his books were for him, his sole passion and purpose. Jack Greene, the janitor, once told me that years ago after Karen Eli Windslow lamazed the presses into finally giving birth to Forbes' second book, Jack had interrupted Forbes in the restroom masturbating. When Forbes came out of the stall he'd been holding his new novel. I don't know if the story is true or not but to Forbes, to be an author was akin to being the Pope except that apparently, sex was OK.

*   *   *   *   *

The metaphorical grenade blew the building apart. I'd thought about throwing myself on it but my stomach wasn't up to it, having already torn itself apart from a bleeding ulcer caused in no small part from my years with the Seaview Center. No, this was the big one and besides, I was enjoying the show.

The building actually stood quite soundly on its five year old foundation. There was no blinding flash of fire, no smoke and no sound outside of the eternally repeating "Oh, my God!"s of the accountants and managers as they exited the building. The line staff, among whom I precariously included myself, exited quietly, almost smugly, into the sunshine of a bright Florida spring morning.

Seaview Behavioral Health or SBH, had beautifully imploded in on itself. The grenade while metaphorical, did it's work with the efficiency and expertise of the Hoover Brothers Destruction Company, Central Florida's premiere destruction company who would later get a chance to demonstrate their abilities when they destroyed the building in a literal sense. The actual destruction was almost as entertaining as the metaphorical one but had the added benefit of being recorded for the climactic sequence of a low budget action film. Interestingly, the film, including the 30 second scene in which the building blew up, made more profit in its first weekend's release than all the building's occupants had earned in the two years prior to its desertion and implosion.

The metaphorical grenade was my idea but everyone who I had shared it with had agreed that it was most appropriate. There had been plenty of time to evacuate prior to the "explosion" but I had chosen to stay to study the intricate inner workings of a self ignited corporate destruction. With a couple of exceptions, I had not been disappointed. It had been artistic to behold, each phase undeniable as death and taxes. Each committee approved, CQI'd, raise it up the flagpole decision unknowingly leading to the inevitable, the bankruptcy bomb.

As I left the building I assessed the situation. Assessment was after all, my job at Seaview. It was a job that I was so well qualified for that my name badge had read in large gold print beneath my name - "Assessment Specialist". I assessed people for a living but didn't see why I couldn't assess other things, like a bicycle, a computer, or my monthly credit card statements - or relationships, or situations. It was all essentially the same process. My assessment of Seaview Behavioral Health Center Incorporated, if I had been able to write it up on Initial Assessment Form number CC222-A1293, would have looked something like this:

1) *Presenting problem: Client has no insight into their problem whatsoever. Firmly in denial.*

2) *Mental status: Generally oriented X3, some occasional confusion regarding which decade we are in.*

3) *Symtomology: Clear split with reality. Poor decision making based on faulty logic, elaborate fantasies and delusional thinking. Contradicts self. Egocentric.*

4) *Client History: Client has history of suicidal gestures.*

5) <u>Lethality</u>: High suicide risk. Motive and access to means to self explosion.

6) <u>Recommendation</u>: Sell film rights of inevitable suicidal explosion to highest bidder.

Where are the Hoover Brothers when you need them?

*   *   *   *   *

If Forbes was the first then Marcus Jones made up the second third of the triumvirate that were my friends. Marcus' reign as my roommate began not too long after the explosion at Seaview and lasted, on and off again, up until the month before I won an Academy Award for Best Documentary. I mentioned his name in my speech just after my mother. My entire speech was this:

"Obviously there is Forbes. Otherwise there's no one in particular to thank other than my mother and Marcus. It is not that I am not thankful, but those that have crossed my path and made it better are no more or less to credit for my theft of this piece of metal than are those

*who made it worse. And to list you all would ultimately
bore you so I offer Mom and Marcus as representative of
everyone."*

The speech was not well received by the few who heard
it but I heard that Marcus liked it. And that's exactly why I'd said
it. My mother had been dead for eleven years. Her role was over
pretty much five or ten minutes after I was born. Her opinion
would have been as hard to obtain eleven years prior to my
speech as it would now and would have mattered less. Mom was
a pale woman with tobacco stained fingers. We never really got
along.

Marcus on the other hand, was easy to get along with
once you knew him, which few people bothered to do. He was a
black man - very black with shiny black skin. He would have
made a good statue, a statue with many interesting stories. He
had served in Vietnam and, while he never actually shot anyone,
had once placed second in the Army's national, annual
marksmanship competition. Perhaps his best story was when,
according to Marcus, he touched President Nixon's hand. At the
beginning of this story, if Marcus were telling it, which he rarely
did, he would point to a spot on his right hand where the actual
contact had been made. Apparently, he did not particularly care
for the President as evidenced by what he said to him as they
touched. It was a simple word that floated up, lost among the

millions of other words that were floating away into space. The crowd at the airport that day was estimated at over 5000. Lots of words were crammed into that space but Marcus' word slipped past all the others and made its way to the President's ears. Marcus himself never heard it. As the President reached out to shake the hands of the crowd leaning over the fence, in particular, as he reach out and touched Marcus' hand, Marcus whispered... "Bang."

When Marcus tells the story, he ends it there with him laughing hysterically. He doesn't tell the rest because he doesn't think the rest is all that funny.

In memory of Marcus and because it didn't match my decor, I painted my Academy Award black and placed it on my coffee table between my genuine black leather recliner and the end of my genuine black leather couch. I knocked it over regularly. More recently, it has turned up missing but I think I know who has it.

*   *   *   *   *

And now, as they say, for the rest of the story, the part that Marcus never tells about his brush with the Presidency. The following information was obtained through my professional assessment upon Marcus' first involuntary commitment to our

Center and related to you in violation of every client confidentiality law in the sunny state of Florida.

Apparently the Secret Service did not appreciate the humor in Marcus' word and from what Marcus told me later, neither did Tricky Dick. According to Marcus, Nixon's eyes rolled back in his head and he nearly had a heart attack. It was from that point on, according to Marcus, that Richard Nixon, knowing he could go at any moment and in order to ensure his place in history, began recording all his conversations. The rest, as they also say, is history. History according to Marcus.

Marcus' part in history was sealed with his being charged with endangering the Presidency and his subsequent arrest. This was all accomplished with the utmost discretion and secrecy. Of the other 4999 civilians standing in the rain at the airport that day, not one knew of Marcus' arrest. Interestingly, not a single name of these 4999 cheering, flag waving Americans has been recorded anywhere. I know this because recently I've had little to do but research useless facts just such as this.

On that particular day, only the names of Marcus Jones and Richard Nixon has history found significant enough to remember.

*   *   *   *   *

Psychiatry is, at best, an imprecise science. It is clearly science in that there are hypothesis, experimentation, and a definite concept of fallibility. Yet nowhere in the wide scope of scientific study is the experimental stage so close to the public. Drugs are developed, manufactured, prescribed and taken without anyone along the way really knowing if and why they will work.

Some drugs work. I've seen people who could hardly speak, gush their life stories as if they were hearing them for the first time themselves. I've seen a woman once convinced that she was the mother of both Jesus Christ and Michael Jackson, once on the proper meds, closing a commodity deal worth over two million dollars. I've seen the blind see and the cripple walk.

But I've also seen the blind stay blind and the crazy stay crazy.

With each new medication the docs would get a little closer, help a few more people, but in the end they still had hardly a clue as to why a certain medication helped a certain person.

Marcus Jones suffered from schizophrenia. Still does.

He shuffled around on Haldol for a while, slept through Prolixin and even stuck through Clozaril while remaining pretty much the same. He got fat and got skinny again. He was impotent for a while, which didn't seem to alter his sex life much. He remained paranoid, quiet and alone.

He looked like a tortured artist only he had little artistic talent to profit from his pain. In my first assessment of him, I had noted that he possessed a "flat affect". Because he often walked through life with the blank exterior, he became the canvas on which others would paint their works of art. To the paranoid among us, he was dangerous. To the primadonnas, he was pitiful. He was the screen on which was projected the fears, prejudices and hopes of anyone he met.

I saw him as constant. What does that say about me?

*   *   *   *   *

Stanc Autoworks produced cars in Germany from 1972 to 1999. Stanc was world renown for the quickest turn around time from concept to sale. "You want the latest? Get a Stanc." proclaimed their billboards. Its been said that Stanc engineers literally rushed from their computers down to the assembly line floor shaking blueprints in their hands at the shop foremen. The foremen snapped up the blueprints, stopped the assembly lines, with all their cars in various stages of construction, and began to manufacture the engineers' latest creations. The first few cars off the line were hybrids, part old models, part new. These were destined to become collector's items and would take in hundreds of thousands at auctions put on for car collectors around the world. Sometimes the hybrid models would work great, sometimes they'd be safe and sometimes they wouldn't. Sometimes, they wouldn't even run.

*   *   *   *   *

Back when Marcus was my client, before he had become my friend and roommate, I once asked him to transcribe, as accurately as possible, what he remembered as having been said at his trial for endangerment of the Presidency. I've listed below what he wrote. Recently, I have taken the liberty to add several additional statements. These were not included as part of the memory of Marcus Jones but instead were recorded as part of the official transcription recorded by Mrs. Jane Francine Fitzgerald who was the court transcriptionist assigned to the trial. I include them for your orientation purposes and to justify the time I spent obtaining the actual transcripts. As I have said, for the last few days, I have been a man with little else to do other than look up articles and old transcripts.

THE STATE VS MARCUS JONES

(Statements in italics are as recollected by Marcus but were not part of the official transcripts)

Charge: Endangerment of the Presidency, 1/27/70

JUDGE: "Mr. Jones, do you understand the charges against you?" (This is one of only two statements attributed to others in the courtroom in which Marcus' memory of the events and the actual court transcription match perfectly. Marcus' memory of his own statements are for the most part, remarkably accurate.)

JUDGE: *"Do you understand that we wish to put you in jail to keep you from telling the President that we plan to have him killed?"*

MARCUS: "No."

JUDGE: *"What? What is it that you do not understand?"*

MARCUS: "Why'd you want to go and kill the President?"

JUDGE: *"Now Marcus, you keep quiet about that or we'll be seeing you soon. Its you or him, take your choice."*

MARCUS: "I ain't gonna kill no president."

JUDGE: *"Take off your clothes Marcus."*

MARCUS: "I don't want to take off my clothes."

JUDGE: *"Take off your clothes Marcus or we'll hurt the President."*

MARCUS: "I don't give a fuck what happens to the President."

JUDGE: *"Take off your clothes Marcus or we will make you hurt the President."*

MARCUS: "Fuck."

Both Marcus and the official transcript agree that at this point Marcus began taking his clothes off and was restrained by security as he got down to his underwear which, as dutifully recorded by Mrs. Fitzgerald, were boxers.

The actual transcripts also included the following statements:

"I assure you Mr. Jones that we have no intention of killing anyone."(Judge Warren) *and "Mr. Jones if you continue to use language like that...* (Judge Warren) and the actual transcripts make no reference whatsoever to anyone killing the President or anyone desiring Marcus to disrobe.

The second statement which Marcus remembered exactly as transcribed in the record was a warning from the Judge - "We will be watching you son, we'll be watching you."

Marcus was eventually found not guilty due to insanity and ordered to mandatory treatment at the Seaview Behavioral Center where he was promptly brought and assessed by an Assessment Specialist by the name of Thomas Little. An average man with unusual luck and an extraordinary fondness for tomatoes.

Who is me. I'm glad to meet you.

Interestingly, despite all the hoopla described above, you will soon see that Nixon would not be the only President who would experience Marcus' sense of humor.

*   *   *   *   *

Evolution is a dark business.

Things must reproduce and then die. Ideas, in the form of accidental mutations, are tried by nature, fail and die. A butterfly with hereof unknown patterns of beautiful colors and shapes is not chosen to mate. It dies along with its uniqueness, its perfect appearance never to be seen again.

The fact that they evolve is only one of many ways businesses are like living creatures. Another is they both leave a lot of waste behind for other organisms to clean up. When it comes to evolution though, organizations and businesses in particular are more like a June bug or the male black widow spider. While a business may occasionally spawn an offspring and survive, its more the exception than the rule. Like the June bug, most businesses die in the process of reproducing.

As the climate changed and another social ice age encroached, Seaview tried its damnedest to adapt but, just like the famous white moths of the countryside of industrialized England, Seaview had to give way to its new, more adept, soot colored brothers and sisters. We couldn't change the way we did things anymore than the white moths could change their color, or the brontosaurus could lose weight or whatever caused it to pack it up and die off. We knew we were the wrong color. We knew we

27

needed to mutate to survive. We just couldn't do a damn thing about it.

Like I said, evolution is a dark business.

*   *   *   *   *

Let me tell you about being crazy.

No, I've never been and I apologize to those of you who have. I'm sure I will not do it justice but words are all I have and to truly understand the events I plan to describe, the reader must understand the mind of the mentally ill. For those of you experienced in this area, feel free to skip this section and move on the more action oriented portion of this book.

Now... let me take a minute of your time and tell you about being crazy.

First of all, what it's not.

It's not being stupid (although some suffering from it are). It's not evil (though some people with it can be). It's not being innocent (although some are). The mentally ill (only the crazy can really call himself or herself crazy) are generally not drooling, knife wielding, steeple climbing, or ax murdering weirdoes. In fact, studies have repeatedly shown that people suffering from schizophrenia are for the most part less violent than the rest of us. They are simply more creative (generally) even

28

when deciding how to knock off their in-laws. It's not romantic, fun, interesting, nor relaxing and it ain't great to be.

Marcus is mentally ill. He's schizophrenic, which is a term I hate, but he doesn't seem to mind it. (My mother had cancer when she was getting old but no one called her an old cancer. At least not to her face.) Marcus has paranoid delusions and hears voices. On really bad days he sees eyeballs on the walls.

He's also a Bulls fan which has more to do with Michael Jordan than mental illness.

Marcus is never sure if I like him.

Despite this, he is one of the best friends I've ever had.

*   *   *   *   *

The 1995 c.12 version of the Stanc Excelsior had the boxy back end found on all 95 Stanc automobiles and a front end with the more stylish, fluid body molding that represented the critically acclaimed, revolutionary design change in the 1996 models. There were only twelve cars on the assembly line the day the changes came down and, true to Stanc tradition, no time was lost finishing them the new way. By the end of the day twelve truly ugly hybrid cars were loaded up on a truck and shipped to a dealership in Titusville, Florida.

Ten of these cars had been located and were already worth over $250,000 each. The death of one of the remaining two 1995 c.12 Stanc Excelsiors was documented on video as part of a high speed car chase and subsequent crash in Ann Arbor. It seems its owner, a Robert Happensac Jr. decided to use the old car his father had given him in a hold up of a local liquor store. His take was $112 and a bottle of tequila. He ended up with a broken leg, a broken collar bone, a nasty cut on his face and ten to fifteen for armed robbery and a variety of other charges. In prison, someone told Robert about the real value of his "old car" and Robert tried to hang himself with his sheets. He was unsuccessful.

He is now an avid reader of Motor Car Today magazine and is scheduled for a parole hearing next January.

The remaining 1995 hybrid has never been located. Somewhere there is an old man or maybe a young dental assistant driving a gold mine. All that and they're probably not getting the oil changed every 3000 miles. Even for carbon monoxide spitting, natural resource eating monstrosities, these machines stand out as being unusually unpleasant to look at and generally run like crap. Why they are worth $250,000 is beyond me. I'd rather have had a Volkswagen and spend a month in a dollar store. Or a bike and a lifetime supply of toilet paper. Or a bus pass and unlimited pizza delivery.

Speaking of toilet paper, what if we came across a culture somewhere that used gold leaf to wipe their behinds and thin soft paper products as jewelry and currency? What if one of us was dumped into that culture with no hope of return, how would we feel about flushing a crap encrusted, 14 carrot dump?

This is how I felt then *and* how I feel now, but there was a time in between however, during the meat (pepperoni?) of this story if you will, that I too purchased a 1995 Stanc c.12 Excelsior. I had upgraded it with tinted, bullet proof glass, a DVD player, a Champaign chiller and seats that vibrated alternating between massaging your back and ass. But... let's take a little more bread before we get to the sausage of our story.

*   *   *   *   *

"The Religion of Randomness" was the title of Forbes Maxwell's fifth book. In it he varied greatly from his proven formula of telling people what they wanted to hear, a fact noticed immediately by everyone from his agent to Jack Greene, the Seaview janitor. Why would Forbes mess with a proven thing? Because he could, he wanted to and being a modestly successful author having made $1,765,677.07 for his publisher, they really had no choice but to let him.

No one wanted him to publish this book. They believed that it wasn't about anything anyone wanted to hear. Forbes didn't care, he wanted to write it anyway. His publishers couldn't have possibly been more wrong.

Half way down page two of the book, Forbes asks "What would the universe look like if it were a totally random event?" He spends most of the rest of the book answering that question. The title was chosen for its alliteration value, the book was never intended to actually be interpreted as a religion.

Alliteration is apparently a powerful thing because after several months of B flat sales, the book would be embraced by the aging black haired, pierced generation. Becoming disenchanted with vampires and fairies, the pale skinned, dark side of Generations X, Y and Z were the first to turn toward "ROAR" -The Religion of Absolute Randomness - for guidance and inspiration. Once they had it, they couldn't let it go. As they were forced into the more traditional roles of parents, accountants and PTA secretaries, it was no longer practical to stay out until 4:00 a.m. wearing black lipstick. They weren't quite ready however, to retire to the suburbs.

They read Forbes' words describing the eddies and pools of time which filled the universe, and gulped it like new age nectar. Perhaps most surprising, at least to me, is that I too would not only nurse at the source of this milk for over-preached minds, but I would become its primary prophet. This would be my second dance with fame.

A dance to a song that has continued to this day. That is, until tomorrow. Tomorrow, I not only plan not to get married but I will also step off the dance floor as the prophet of the hour.

Maybe.

*   *   *   *   *

The first time I became famous, it came up like a weed among my tomatoes.

I was staring at bottles of Goldshlagger, Yegermister and all the other trendy liquors that lined the shelves behind the bar. In The Hideaway, there were really only three things to look at, the bottles, square white napkins or a 19-inch TV showing a baseball game with no sound. The Reds were trouncing the Mets.

"I was a ditch digger for the government." Norm blurted out, never taking his eyes from the ball game. I knew he was speaking to Marcus and myself because we were the only other customers in the building.

I've already mentioned Norm. Norman Hurst was nearly 80 and had shrunk as is the custom of old people, to the point where his feet dangled from the barstool, not even coming close to reaching the floor. While I considered Norm the last of my three true friends, I highly doubt he saw it the same way. Everyone was, to Norm, simply getting in his way and generally speaking, the world would be better off if everyone other than the people on TV, just disappeared. Norm was also fairly far along the road to the Alzheimer Inn. The place where people check in but can't leave because they can't remember where they put their keys.

"I shook hands with the President." Marcus tossed out like an empty beer cup onto the ball field. On the field someone was paid to pick it up. Here the fact just blew away.

For my part, I didn't say anything. To that point, I had been intent on peeling the label from my Paxon Beer in a single piece. As you know, I already knew Marcus' President story but it's not everyone who has a complete Paxon label.

No one spoke and, silence returned to its place and my label was liberated from its oppressive container. The Mets mounted a comeback.

Finally, Norm, still clutching his full draft said, "I dug a ditch under the White House once." He turned and looked at me. "There's tunnels under there you know."

"Yeah." Marcus said.

I wasn't sure if he meant "Yeah, no kidding?", "Yeah, I knew that." or "Yeah, whatever." I think it was the latter.

I can't leave a weed alone. I have to pluck it out by its roots. It's a character fault of which I'm aware and have accepted, although others have not. Often, after having yanked one up, I find that it wasn't a weed at all. It might have been a flower worth looking at - if I hadn't killed it.

"Norm, there are no tunnels under the White House." I could hear the ripping noises as I tore up the little roots of Norm's claim but I pressed on. "Do you know what a security risk that would be? And if there were, which there aren't, they'd have filled them up years ago. They just can't leave open access to the President like that. Too many fronts to watch or flanks to defend or Secret Servicemen to deploy or something I'm sure."

"I just said there were ditches and that I dug 'em. I make no comment on their current state of repair." Norm gulped his beer down, turning his eyes up across the ceiling and back to the game. "Don't get snotty with me."

"I'm sorry." I said trying to replant the moment and get it to grow again. "It just doesn't make sense to me is all."

Norm didn't say anything.

"Norm, I'm sorry. Tell me about the tunnels" I begged.

His gaze remained fixed on the game. The silence returned.

Several minutes later Marcus said, "Eisenhower snuck one of his daughters out through one of those tunnels after she got married."

"What?" I said. "How do you know that?"

"Something I read." He went on, "they sent a couple of cars out front to distract the press. Worked like a charm."

"The first ones were built back years ago when they first built the thing." Norm stared forward. "They were small ones, maybe three or four feet across. There were only one or two but they weren't much use. They rebuilt the building back in the late 1800's. And made it all steel inside, the whole thing had been rotting away and getting eaten up by termites. They added more tunnels then and they were bigger. You could move supplies in and out in case of an emergency."

I sat there slack jawed. There had been more words there than I had ever heard Norm speak at any one time. His focus was now clearly on the ball game but I could detect a smugness just below the surface that said, "You all think I'm a senile old man but I'm not". After a minute, he got up and left, forgetting to pay for his beer.

I let him go knowing he'd be back in a half-hour or so looking for help finding his car. I turned to Marcus.

"Do you think they're still there?"

"I know they are."

"How can you be so sure?"

"They are always there." Marcus turned and looked over shoulder. "CIA, FBI, they're all there. Watching through the TV."

"Marcus, you've lost me again. There's no one following you." We had had this conversation before.

"Really?" Marcus was genuinely surprised.

"Really." I turned my attention back to the game. "The Mets suck."

"The Reds suck."

We'd had this conversation before too. I patted Marcus on the shoulder and got up to go find Norm.

*   *   *   *   *

It wasn't until recently that I knew that not only did Norm really work in construction in the Washington, DC area, he was fairly well known among the bulldozer types of his day. He had designed a portable structure that doubled the speed at which a ditch for sewer lines could be built and in the process, increased the safety factor tenfold for the workers actually doing the work. He had two other patents as well. One for a mini-hole drilling machine and another for a machine that, despite the fact that I've read the original proposal, I still don't know exactly what it does.

None of his machines are in use today and apparently, they were so specialized at the time that they never really provided Norm with any significant income.

Norm had also been married.

His wife of thirty years left him the day after she won 2.2 million dollars in the Florida lottery. Norm had already begun his slippery slide into Alzheimer's. Emma paid the Golden Age Retirement Home enough money to take care of Norm for one year... and then she left.

She died three years later in a car accident on her way back from the South Florida Indian Casino. Her three kids from a previous marriage inherited her money, invested it in a family run import-export business dealing in black market goods from Cuba. They couldn't get along and the business went completely under when the youngest turned in his siblings to the federal authorities in a plea bargain deal.

The Golden Age Retirement Home was banking on Norm passing relatively quickly. They recently tried to have him removed but I had my attorneys look over the original contract that Emma had drawn up. I am happy to report that even though Norm has outlived the single year Emma so graciously paid for, Golden Age is stuck with him at least for a while.

*　　*　　*　　*　　*

It had been two months since Seaview had gone bankrupt and I had lost my job. I was quickly eating though my anemic savings. To make ends meet, I had invited Marcus to stay with me. He pitched in a portion of his monthly benefit money toward rent and I let him sleep on the couch which, according to Marcus, was "a little better" than the shelter.

I'd agreed not to turn on the TV. There was no need for the CIA to know where Marcus was.

You would have thought that our casual conversation at the bar about the tunnels under the White House would have faded as fast as whoever won the baseball game or as fast as Norm's ability to remember his keys.

It didn't.

The Golden Age Retirement Home was only a mile away and Norm drove his 1972 Buick to The Hideaway for one beer each evening which took him about two hours to drink. That was his life. If my brain was a bit shuffled at times, Norm's cards were spread out like a game of 52 pick-up. Where Marcus was usually there with only occasional waves of delusions, Norm was usually confused with only occasional waves of being there. As for me, I guess I'm usually lucid with only occasional waves of gas.

Norm's pronouncements about the tunnels under the White House rang true enough to warrant a closer look. My real interest originally was whether Norm's brain had correctly filed this nugget of information rather than in the accuracy of the information itself. A quick trip to the library convinced me that there was probably something to what he had said. As I sat and read the stories regarding the White House, which were for the most part most easily found in children's books for some reason, the topic of the tunnels began to intrigue me. The idea that there would be tunnels under the White House made some level of sense to me. It also seemed logical that they hadn't been destroyed. While it was not surprising that personally I knew nothing of them, I was somewhat surprised that there was so little information easily available regarding them. It was at this precise moment that the serenity of my tomato garden was put into question. A weed of an idea sprouted in my mind and it wouldn't go away. More importantly, neither Norm, Marcus or myself had absolutely anything else to do. Before I really even had a chance to consider what it would be like, there we were, on our way to Washington, DC. A road trip with all the makings of a bad comedy.

*   *   *   *   *

The Orlando Sentinel – Local and State, page 1:

Orange County – Police in downtown Orlando closed a section of Robinson Street last night due to what is being called a "natural phenomenon" in the alley between Robinson and White streets. Lt. Al Divers of OPD stated: "We have what appears to be some type of natural occurring event which we don't understand at this time. This is clearly not a sinkhole. I want to stress that there does not appear to be any danger at this time but the public will be kept from the area until we get a better idea as to what we are dealing with." Divers went on to say that the Department had contacted the University Of Central Florida Natural Sciences Department for assistance. Commuters can expect delays in the area for the next few days and are encouraged to take alternate routes.

This was the second article I was able to dig up during my recent snooping in the Forbes Maxwell Memorial Library. At the time this was written they obviously hadn't made the link between the two missing boys – Dante and Jose – and the "natural occurring event" described above but they were indeed very much related. It would only be a matter of days after this story was published before the Robinson Street alley would become very famous. Not so coincidentally, the rise to fame of this "natural occurring event" would coincide almost exactly with my own.

*   *   *   *   *

President Frank Fisher was Commander in Chief during the majority of events I am describing here. Today however, he is no longer President and may possibly be among the guests for my impending wedding. How many people can get away with standing up a former President? I told you I was famous.

*   *   *   *   *

But that is now and this is then.

I was sitting on a tautly made, orange double bed, exercising my index finger on the remote bolted to the nightstand which was bolted to the floor next to the bed. Marcus was sitting on the other double bed and had pulled the matching orange curtains aside and was staring into the parking lot of the R.J. Motel. He had spent the previous two hours engrossed in the latest book by my old friend Forbes. "The Religion of Absolute Randomness" was at this point, still a book that very few people, including me, had paid any notice.

Norm came out of the bathroom, still working on zipping his pants.

I ran into a string of channels with blue backgrounds and filled with scrolling text describing the hotel's breakfast menu. I turned off the TV. Outside it was raining that hard throbbing type of rain with peaks and valleys of water shoved downward from a flannel gray sky. Yawning, I looked around the room for something to kill the time.

Marcus kept watching the parked cars stand still and Norm continued to work on his zipper. This was pretty much the way my day had gone. The eight hour drive from Orlando had taken us twelve and seemed like twenty. Marcus and I had switched off driving duties as Norm rode silently in the back. The conversation had had all the excitement and pace of a wait in line for the water flume at an amusement park on a 96 degree summer afternoon - just let it be over. As soon as we got outside of Fayetteville, N.C., we stopped for a bucket of chicken and found a room. Now the lack of conversation was beginning to have its effect on me.

"Are they out there?" I asked Marcus.

"Who?"

"The FBI."

"No." he snorted, "Why would the FBI be outside this hotel room?"

Sometimes he was there, sometimes he wasn't. You never knew with Marcus.

"So what do you think of that book?" I tried again.

"Just avoid channel 32." Marcus said.

You had to love him.

"The book's good." He nodded and rapped it with his knuckles. "According to this, billions of little strange pockets of oddness and coincidence are to be expected in a state of utter randomness. Some day one hundred monkeys will type War and Peace. Some day someone I know will win the lottery. Some day you will meet, fall in love with and marry a model."

At that particular moment, I was reaching over and helping Norm with his zipper and the chance of me meeting a model seemed utterly remote, even with the billions of "pockets of coincidence."

"The point is," he continued, now quoting directly from the book "that chance can explain our world equally as well as any religion, mystic and theological belief out there today.' "

"King James has always worked for me." Norm said as he reached into the nightstand and pulled out the small pocket Bible the hotel had provided for just such occasions. "And things being equal and all, I think I'll stick with what I know to be true." After this pronouncement Norm promptly stole the Book and placed it his bag. As you will see later, this oxymoronic innocent theft, will turn out to be a pocket of coincidence of truly preposterous proportions.

Just moments before I was bemoaning the silence, now I was witnessing a petty theft in the middle of a theological debate. One second you're sweating out the line, the next you're flying down the flume. Go figure.

*   *   *   *   *

The baggage which has been selected (either naturally like Darwin's brain bag or supernaturally like Matthew, Luke or John's) to be the carrying case of our most valued possessions remains the most misunderstood and miraculous package known to man. Our skull, at a centimeter or so thick, has done an admirable job of protecting its contents from hairy armed baggage handlers from primitive times up until today. That's a good thing because it has only a limited ability to repair itself and the mushy stuff inside is extremely valuable. Especially to its owner.

Although self repairs on hardware are nearly impossible, our brain's ability to create alternative pathways within itself and to jump across connections and make new linkages have made it extremely useful for things like deciding if it's time to turn our fried eggs or to come up with advertising campaigns and Silly Putty.

As valuable as these things may be, they are socks and underwear compared to the primary content of our brain bags - our personality. If we were to check into a hotel, we'd let the maids go through our dirty socks and ripped underwear but we'd want to lock up our personality in the hotel safe. That however, would be hard to do. It's not the nerves and chemicals that make it up, it's the space in between. (Kind of like locking up the space between our toothbrush and our antiperspirant). You can search the entire brain bag and never touch the personality but there it is, spewing out of us at every possible opportunity.

*   *   *   *   *

WASHINGTON, DC

I checked into Hotel Washington on 15th Avenue shortly after 9:00 p.m. After I had made it to my room and tipped the bellhop, I immediately walked down the hall to let Marcus and Norm in and led them up the back stairs to our room.

"Spring in Washington," Norm was saying, "a most enjoyable experience."

Norm was glowing like a pregnant woman. Somehow the trip or the city itself seemed to invigorate him. His bushy eyebrows that usually lay heavy over half open eyes bounced up and down and around the room. He looked out the window.

"See that there? That's the Treasury Building." Norm pointed to the building across the street. "Back years ago, during the war when mostly women worked there, there was a Treasury boss that...you know... with hundreds of employees. He got nearly fifty of them pregnant."

"Oh, the good old days, huh?" I remarked.

"No, not any better by no means. Things were just simpler." He said still staring out the window. "Just simpler is all."

"Norm, you think the tunnel is still there?" Marcus asked. "Does it run straight from here under the Treasury building?"

We had avoided talking about it nearly the entire trip, as if we were afraid of someone listening. What was probably more accurate was that we were afraid that if we talked about it, somehow we'd ruin the chances of it being true. Somehow the words would float into space as Marcus' word did at the airport years ago and somehow it would alter the ether in such a way that the tunnel would disappear before we even had a chance to see it. Another postulate in the geometry of the human brain - an empty bag creates its own contents.

"I don't know." Norm answered, "Hotel's in the same spot. Treasury building's still there."

"Norm, where did you guys park the car?" I asked.

The familiar dazed look of confusion crossed his face and I turned to Marcus and shot him a "he probably has his underwear on backwards and you're asking him about nuclear physics" kind of smile. He understood my point.

"You brought him." Marcus said. "And he's got more there than we know." He tapped his finger against his head.

"More where?" Norm asked.

"More here." I motioned to the beverage bar. "You want something to drink Norm?"

"Got a beer?"

"Sure we do." I said and cracked open a can and handed it to him.

*   *   *   *   *

It had been so, so very simple.

Norm led us down to the ground floor lobby, down a spiral staircase and into an empty ballroom. At the end of the ballroom was a chameleon service door, the kind that guests pass without thinking about even though it remains plainly in view.

The service door wasn't locked and it opened up into another perpendicular hallway that was clearly "back of the house" with often painted walls of concrete and cinder block. This was a place that was cleaned by a guy in hip boots and a hose rather than by a soft pink clad housekeeper with a Bissell.

A short distance down the hall to our right was a small unlocked panel which was used to service the elevators on the west side of the hallway we'd just left. We climbed through the panel and into an elevator shaft filled with whirring motors and spinning cables. Located inconspicuously on the floor next to the primary motor was a small hatch. There had obviously been a lock on the hatch at sometime in the not so distance past but now the latch lifted easily and unhindered. We crawled in.

If moments before Norm had opened his mouth, back when we sat at our stools at The Hideaway drinking happy hour drafts, watching the ball game and contemplating the physics of a rising fastball, if in that naive moment, I were to have closed my eyes and pictured what a tunnel under the White House would have looked like, I would have been extremely close to what our flashlights found. Lots of dark and dirt decorated with cobwebs.

There were several large pipes taking up nearly the entire left side of the squarish passage, leaving only enough room for us to move in single file along the crumbling brick wall on the right. Something I wouldn't have included in my cliché tunnel was the choking dryness that pervaded the air. We were only a few steps in but each step had resulted in a mini mushroom cloud of dust exploding around our feet that seemed to suck in and swallow any sound that might have been created.

We stopped for a moment to gain our bearings and get accustomed to the claustrophobic feel of the place.

"Tom, look." Marcus said pointing the beam of his flashlight ahead down the passageway.

Ahead of us in the dust on the floor, we could clearly make out a number of foot prints overlapping in both directions.

I'm no Indian Guide and quit Cub Scouts because I though our scout master was creepy but even I could tell that these weren't old prints. Someone regularly traveled this tunnel.

"Well?" Norm asked.

"Well what?"

"Well what are we going to do?"

"How the hell am I supposed to know?" I said "Why are you looking at me?"

"I," Norm stated in a patient voice. "am a senile old man and Marcus is crazy as a loon which leaves you in charge of the facility."

I looked at Marcus and he shrugged. I considered pointing out the fact that this logic had been lost when it had come to the decisions regarding where to eat or who had to sleep on the couch or which radio station to listen to or any other decision since the whole adventure had begun, but I let it pass and pushed past Marcus and headed up the tunnel.

The tunnel was a wonderful place. As I moved forward, a private smile skipped across my face and parked itself like a kid smugly plopping into his dad's easy chair. This was the adventure that I didn't even know I was looking for. I realized I wasn't there to take care of Marcus or Norm. I was there for me. For the rush of it. The footprints ahead were leading me somewhere. It really didn't matter where but it would be good. It would be good because it was different than my pitiful Cheerio and skim milk existence. I looked down several side tunnels that disappeared into darkness and felt the sensation of fear creep through my toes. Damn it felt good.

I stopped for a moment, taking a mental Polaroid. This is a technique I used to suggest to my clients all the time. I wanted to freeze the moment. Preserve it in my mind for others less kind. For a moment, I wasn't a pudgy balding man past his prime, for this moment anyway, I was adventuring like few people could imagine. I was a bearded climber bivouacked at high camp on Everest and a diver among the sharks of the Great Barrier Reef. I was a diva about to shock the world with her talent a moment before her first concert. I was a shuttle crew member listening to his own breath waiting for the shock of lift off. These moments happened so rarely anymore that I wanted to grab it and cradle it in my hands, watching it like a school boy holding a fire fly on a hot summer night.

"Tom?"

"Yea Norm?"

"Let's hurry."

"There's nothing to be afraid of. Enjoy the moment."

"I have to go to the bathroom."

*   *   *   *   *

Without cameras, servants and gobs of men and women in business suits, the depths of the White House, with the exception of the capitalization, feels a lot like the home of any other rich, highly powerful, elite person in a capitalistic world. The floors creak, there are dark corners and even a few places in need of dusting. There are doorways with little scratches from where someone bumped them with a serving tray or when moving a piece of furniture that belonged to a dead President.

If you look real close, you'll see an extension cord here or there, some ankle height lines where the dog scratched the molding and even a finger print or two. Just a regular house that happens to team with security and tourists.

After exiting the dimly lit tunnels, we entered the home of our nation's leader into a brightly lit bathroom, through a panel located behind a toilet. Apparently, even the Commander in Chief can't remember to put the seat down. In his defense, it didn't look like the kind of bathroom that regularly hosted the Presidential behind.

The fact that we had entered the White House through the outhouse prompted Marcus to remark that we were very fortunate that the tunnel had ended in such a private place that thankfully, had not been in recent use. It prompted me to remark that this probably was not the first time crap was coming in rather than going out.

And it prompted Norm to have a bowel movement.

Things have a way of working out.

*　　　*　　　*　　　*　　　*

A twig of a woman spun into the room, twisting the lock shut all in one urgent motion. She turned to face us, finally noticing our three, dusty bodies still packed around the commode.

"Hi" I said.

"Hi" Marcus said.

"Hi" Norm said.

She stood there frozen, her eyes darting from Norm to me to Marcus and back to Norm. The small yellow puddle forming slowly on the floor between her shiny red heels made it clear what she had expected to do and it wasn't to see us.

Mission accomplished.

We all stood there, with the exception of Norm who was still sitting, concentrating on the task at hand.

Marcus broke the silence. "Hello?"

As if the sound removed the spell that our presence had over her, the woman reached back, turned the knob and swung her body around and out the door, her heels clicking down the hallway like Morse code. It would be just a matter of seconds before they would know that we were there and our little adventure would come to an arresting end.

Without speaking, Marcus grabbed Norm by one shoulder while I grabbed him by the other dragging him, still pulling up his pants, back into the tunnel. As we hurried back toward the elevator shaft, I listened for the sounds I was sure that I would hear – voices yelling, sirens, perhaps the growls and intimidating barks of guard dogs.

We heard nothing. The arid, dusty air seemed to soak up and swallow any sound like a snake gulping down whole prey. When we arrived at the exit we had still not seen nor heard any sign of pursuit. In the elevator, on the way up to our room, my euphoria regarding our escape was tempered by the realization that the libraryish woman who had spotted us, had seen us clearly. And we were a hard group to forget. Furthermore, I'd left the ultimate smoking gun when I had checked into the room under my own name. We had left a trail of bread crumbs the size of whole loaves leading right to our door.

When we arrived at the room I plopped on the bed awaiting the inevitable. Marcus began gathering up his clothes and cigarettes and stuffed them in Norm's old suitcase.

"Its no use." I said finally "They will find us."

"No," Marcus corrected, "they will find you. You checked in as a single didn't you?"

"Yea. So?"

"Good." He said as he clicked the case shut. "So, love ya man but me and Norm are gettin' the hell out of here."

"But she saw us all." I said

"What she saw was a white guy, an old guy and a black guy. The white guy, you," he said pointing, "she'll be able to describe well enough to trace back here. The cop will ask her 'What'd the black guy look like ma'am?' and she'll say 'Well he was, ya know, black'.

"How you think I gone all this time without getting' tracked down by the FBI. One good thing about being crazy and black is that those are the only two words rich white folks can think of to describe you."

I saw his point.

"What about Norm?" I asked.

"Same thing." Marcus responded pulling Norm by the arm toward the door. "In that little woman's memory he looked like an 'Old Guy'. OK, an 'Old Guy Taking a Crap' but that's it."

They were already out the door.

I jumped up and yelled down the hallway. "Who do I say I was with?"

Marcus yelled back. "Tell 'em the truth. You were with some crazy black guy and some old senile guy."

"Bye Tom." Norm smiled and waved and they both disappeared down the stairway.

*   *   *   *   *

I ordered room service.

I watched a black and white movie with Jimmy Stewart in it.

I read.

I went to bed.

The phone never rang. The knock on the door never came.

*   *   *   *   *

When I woke up I looked up at the ceiling and created a mental list of possible reasons I was not in jail:

1) The woman never told anyone she saw us.

2) They didn't know about the tunnel and, rather than following our path to the hotel, they spent the night watching security videos trying to figure out where we came from and how we'd gotten out.

3) The woman did tell someone but for some reason they didn't believe her.

4) They had me pegged and were currently watching me to see if they could figure out what I was up to.

I wasn't sure which of these made the most sense but just in case it was the last one, I ordered "Star Whores" from the menu of adult pay for view titles and walked down to the gift shop and picked up a paperback copy of *Catcher In The Rye*.

*   *   *   *   *

If they didn't have me, it was just a matter of time before they did. Or so I thought. It would only be a matter of time before my credit card reached its limit so clearly, the only logical course of action was to help speed up the process. The wheels of justice skid along painfully slow when you're broke and waiting for the inevitable.

*   *   *   *   *

I decided I'd wear a suit for this adventure. In keeping with Marcus' logic, I decided the best way to lay siege to the halls of the seat of power run by white shirted, late middle age white men, was to look like one. I owned only one blue double breasted suit, having long ago sold my others to the consignment store. It fit well enough so I clipped my old Seaview ID on the pocket to complete my disguise.

I looked exactly like me.

Getting to the tunnel was as easy as the first time. No one even looked twice as I passed into the elevator shaft and back into the tunnel.

I made my way back through the brown dark air, back toward the White House, fully expecting to be accosted, roughed up and arrested by close shaven Secret Service agents.

Nothing happened.

Again, I opened the panel behind the guest toilet and entered the bathroom. No alarms. No sirens. Nothing.

Personally, I have never believed that there was any type of a CIA plot involved in the assassination of John or Bobby Kennedy. There are no UFOs stored in some remote southwestern Air Force base. These urban myths simply cannot be true. Our over fed, bloated government mires its feet so deep in bureaucratic mud that it can't even detect a bald intruder taking a piss in the White House sink (a symbolic gesture on my part), much less orchestrate the kind of coordination it would take to pull the wool over the eyes of all the media and the entire American public.

I combed what hair I had left and looked at myself in the mirror. I decided that if my government would not come to me, I'd go to it. I opened the door and stepped, uninvited, into the halls of the home of the President of the United States. I had been here, been seen and left yet here I was again, the very next day, coming though the very same tunnel.

One urban myth I have changed my mind about is the possibility of Kennedy sneaking in women for executive hanky-panky. That was one, given where I was currently standing and what I would have done in JK's shoes, now seemed well within the limits of possibility.

I pushed open the bathroom door and stepped into the hallway with the same feeling as a first time bungee jumper, hang glider or seventh grade boy leaning forward for his first kiss – the certainty that something bad is going happen accompanied by the inability to stop one's self from taking the plunge.

The hall was empty.

It occurred to me that since I hadn't really planned on making it this far, I really didn't have a plan at all. I decided that I would walk to the end of the hallway, wherever it may lead and to whomever it may lead me to. Then I'd turn around and return to the bathroom. Not much of a plan, but daring enough to make my palms sweat.

I made an effort to walk down the broad hallway with my back straight, trying to exude a sense of purpose. Making the first left, I almost bumped into a man and woman standing outside what seemed to be an office door. They looked at me and I nodded as I continued past.

Inside, my heart was slapping one hundred high fives a second with every other muscle of my body. After another left, I continued down a short empty hallway. Ahead, around yet another left turn, I could hear voices.

As I had been walking, a ray of hope had started to grow. A ray made up of thoughts that I may actually be able to pull off this stunt. Now, as I turned the corner, the mushrooms of self-assurance and confidence that had sprouted like a carpet in the darkness of the certainty of failure, started to wither and die.

Now I felt fear for the first time. The freedom that certain failure had provided now was replaced with the anxiety of hope. I tried to focus on maintaining my purposeful appearance. A woman stepped out of an office, her head down reading a paper. As we approached each other, she looked up. We made eye contact for a moment and she dropped her head and continued reading.

Turning left again, I returned to the same hallway from where I had started. I heard footsteps behind me. Just as I was about to return to the bathroom and the tunnel, I turned.

We must have both realized at the same moment that we had seen each other before. This was the same woman who had seen us the previous day.

"Oh my God." She whispered.

*　　　*　　　*　　　*　　　*

"Excuse me. I need to use the restroom." I said it as if it were the most normal of statements.

She was attractive in a mousy, librarian sort of way. I figured that if she screamed, I even might have been able to convince the first few people who came running that she was having a nervous breakdown. The fact that she appeared to be on the verge of one would have made it an easy sell.

"You're... you're not supposed to be here." She stammered. " Who are you? What are you doing here?"

"I know. I'm sorry I startled you. I was just leaving."

I stepped past her into the bathroom and closed the door. I didn't even bother to lock it. I slid the panel to the side and stepped into the tunnel. After watching it snap back into place, I started back down toward the hotel.

Once again, I fully expected a serious number of Secret Service suits to greet me at the other end.

Once again, I was greeted by no one and returned to my room alone.

*   *   *   *   *

I awoke the next morning to a knock on the door. A bellman handed me an envelope and turned back down the hallway. Apparently, he knew better than to expect a tip from someone who slept in his clothes.

The outside of the envelope was cream white except for my name written in a feminine hand in blue ink. Inside was a card with a picture of the White House in spring. Inside the card it read, "Meet me for breakfast. The McDonalds on Pennsylvania. Tomorrow. 8:00 a.m."

Which left me a day to kill.

I showered, changed my clothes and headed out into the diesel smells of the city. The sky was bluer than I'd remembered.

I spent the day as a tourist. The Washington Monument. The Lincoln Memorial. The Capital Building. I was an exemplary member of my herd. Moving from one attraction to the next when I was told, listening attentively when my guides spoke and nodding approvingly at the sacred symbols and relics of my government.

That day, on the edge of a canyon deeper than I could have seen or realized at the time, was one of the happiest days of my life.

I wished Marcus and Norm could have been there.

I arrived back at my hotel room and attempted to pay for another night at the front desk only to find it had been prepaid. In fact, the bill for the next three nights had been paid. Not overly surprised, I returned to my room content to go to bed early and ride my little dingy of fate to wherever it was going to take me.

$$*\qquad*\qquad*\qquad*\qquad*$$

I woke up at 6:30 a.m., showered, shaved and caught a cab in front of the hotel. He dropped me off at McDonalds at 7:30 a.m.

Miss Mousy wasn't anywhere to be seen. The place was fairly crowded but I had no problem finding a seat to enjoy my coffee and Egg McMuffin.

"Good morning Tom." A woman's voice slipped quietly but firmly over my newspaper. I lowered it like a curtain in reverse, revealing the source, starting from the top of her head, down her face, her neck to her arms leaning comfortably on the table.

It was not Miss Mousy.

This woman was beautiful in a simple way. Her hair was pulled back from her face in a pony tail. She wore a baseball cap with a Washington Wizard's logo. She had a comfortable, familiar look, like somebody's sister, the wife of a friend. Although she was clearly in her late forties maybe even early fifties, she was very fit and her youthful clothes did not look out of place. Small crow's feet framed a makeup-less face. She smiled and held out a hand.

"I'm Colleen."

I shook it. It was moist. And warm. And soft.

I noticed a bike locked to a parking sign outside the window.

"Yours?" I asked.

"Yes. It's faster than walking and cheaper than cabs but mainly I do it to keep in shape."

"It's working."

"Thank you." She smiled again for a moment as she leaned forward cupping her hands around her coffee cup. She looked up. "Who are you Thomas Little and what were you doing in the White House and what do you want?"

"Who are you?" I replied immediately wishing I had something more witty.

She left my question hang as if I'd never asked it. She looked directly at me awaiting my reply to her original questions. For my part, I really would have liked to tell her everything but I wasn't sure I really knew the answers.

"Let me help." She began. "Your name is Thomas Little. You live in Orlando, Florida and as far as I can tell, are currently unemployed."

I nodded.

"You spent 15 years of your life working for a nonprofit mental health center and you've never been married. Your mother's name was Carrie Garner and your father was also named Thomas. You were an only child and you are left handed."

"You must have quite the staff." I said.

"Found it all on the internet."

"You found out I was left handed on the internet?"

"No. I guessed that by the way you're holding your cup."

I set my coffee down.

"So," She said, "Am I right? And why were you and your buddies in the White House bathroom?"

"It's really not that complicated." I said. "I came here because an old man who can't even remember where he parks his car told me that, when he was young, he had worked on tunnels under the White House. He was going to come regardless. So being as I was unemployed and had nothing better to do, I came with him to see if it was true."

"To keep an eye on him?"

"That too."

65

"Where is he now?"

"He left."

"And your other friend?" She asked.

"A crazy black man."

"I don't suppose you'd give me their names?"

"You don't know?"

"No, I don't."

"Then, no, I won't."

"Both left for Florida?"

"Yes."

She blew on her coffee, sipped it and looked out the window.

"You do this a lot?" I asked.

"Do what?"

"Ride your bike into the city."

"When I can." She said.

She looked back at me. Now it was my turn to look out the window.

"You're married aren't you?" I asked.

"Yes." She rubbed her finger where her wedding band normally circled it.

"And…you're not particularly happy right now are you?"

"And how do you know so much?" She asked.

"It was my job remember? I ask questions. I used to get paid for assessing that kind of thing."

There were probably several thousand reasons our conversation should have been tense. There were several thousand reasons I should have been afraid. But I wasn't. Our pauses seem natural, comfortable.

"Can I ask you one more thing?"

"Why not." she said.

"How is it that the First Lady of the United States is riding her bike alone to McDonalds for breakfast?"

"When did you know?"

"I wasn't sure… until now."

*   *   *   *   *

The difference between a fictional world and the real world is that in movies and books, men know when to shut up. In reality, our mouths become waterfalls of stupidity.

"I wasn't sure …until now." was my summit. The rest of the conversation was a fumbling cascade of Niagara like proportions. When I was younger and more motivated, I debated the debate team, toasted the toastmasters and trained the trainers. Even now, in most cases I do a passable job of passing verbiage. However, when I recognized who this woman really was, I started falling all over myself.

She understandably wanted to see if I was a stalker slash assassin slash terrorist. The upside is that being a bored, unemployed man didn't compare unfavorably. So despite my ineptitude, when we finally parted company that morning, it was on good terms.

*   *   *   *   *

Her name was Mrs. Colleen Fisher. She was married to the President of the United States and it turns out that Norm's tunnel had been her "link to sanity". She would slip out occasionally and ride her bike or go shopping. She'd go to little league games, county fairs and even caught a Redskin's game once.

The woman we had run into in the bathroom, Miss Mousy, was really Lisa Loenthou, Mrs. Fisher's personal assistant. Even Lisa did not know about the tunnel but she did know enough apparently to not ask questions when the First Lady would disappear from time to time. No one knew. Even the President himself had no idea.

I would find out all this later. At the time, the question for both of us was... what to do now?

Was it safe for her to use the tunnel or was I going to toss my story up like a jump-ball among the talk show seven footers?

Was she going to turn me in? And what about Norm and Marcus? Certainly she could find out who they were and locate them if she tried hard enough.

She asked me my intentions and I told her, truthfully, that I didn't know but promised her I represented no danger. Her secret was safe as long as she wished to keep it.

The fact that she was depressed was clear to me. Her decision that day to put her trust in me was not an endorsement of my trustworthiness. It was simply surrender. She looked tired. I imagined her life was like that of an actress where the movie lasted four years, eight if the President got re-elected.

She was smart enough and powerful enough of a woman to have dealt with me. She simply chose not to. The easiest decision is to not make one. Everything has an end, even if we do nothing to more toward it.

We finished breakfast around nine, cleaned off our table and walked outside to her bike.

She had chosen to leave all the obvious questions unanswered. And that was answer enough for me.

"See you around Tom."

"See you later Mrs. Fisher."

"Please," she rolled her eyes and finally smiled again "I'm not *that* much older than you. Call me Colleen."

"See you around Colleen."

She slid onto the bike, waved and took off into the capital morning traffic.

*   *   *   *   *

For a while, I was content with a parallel course of non-action. If it was good enough for a Yale educated First Lady, then it was good enough for me. And besides, she seemed so… nice. She was a nice woman. And sad. Letting things go would be best.

The more I thought about it however, the more I felt that there was something not satisfactory about her solution. Like those weight loss plans that require you to leave a bite on your plate. There was no closure, no sense of completion. They just left you a little hungry.

I returned to my room that morning and starting packing my bags when I remembered that "they" had prepaid two more nights for me. Not one to condone government waste, I decided I would stay and see a little more of our great Capital. Since I was continuing my civic education and considering I had already visited the home of both the Legislative and Judicial branches of our governmental tree, there was only one branch left for me to climb out upon – the Executive Branch. I was off to the White House for an "official" tour.

As I moved among the hallways and history of the world's most famous home, I found myself looking backwards, around corners and just about everywhere other than where our guide was pointing.

I was looking for her.

Although it is not unheard of for the First Lady to greet White House tour groups, it *was* highly unusual. Given her current state of mind, it seemed even more unlikely than usual.

Yet here I was. Out on a limb and looking for her. Isn't it a fascinating phenomenon how we can engage in purposeful action while not allowing our conscious mind to be aware of it? "Wow. I shouldn't be drinking this strawberry milk shake. What am I thinking? What the hell, it's almost gone now anyway."

So why was I looking to catch another glimpse of the First Lady of the United States? If I had let myself think about it at the time, it would have worked something like this: Maybe if I saw her, I could talk to her. Maybe if I talked to her more, she would talk more to me. And maybe if she talked more to me, she would like me more. Maybe if she liked me more... she'd leave her husband, cast aside her celebrity, marry an out of shape trespasser and live happily ever after on his unemployment benefits.

But mercifully, the tour ended before I even realized what I was up to.

Returning to my room, I collapsed into a shallow nap. I had come to Washington with just the clothes on my back and I was beginning to feel like I would be leaving in my underwear.

*   *   *   *   *

Orlando Sentinel – Missing boys linked to "Black hole"
– Authorities are now confident that the earlier disappearance of two boys, Dante Garcia and Jose Murphy, is directly related to the "black hole" phenomenon off of Robinson Street. Authorities have completely restricted the area from everyone with the exception of scientists from the Florida University, Florida State University and the University of Central Florida.

An anonymous official has described the phenomenon as a "hole in space" saying it is the "…strangest thing I have ever seen. We've got the best professors and experts in the state in here and none of them know what to make of it. Objects can enter the hole

but nothing comes out. Its amazing." The hole is
reportedly nearly four feet in diameter and seemingly
suspended in space. There is no word as to how long it
has been there or as to exactly what it is.

Police confirmed that the two officers reported
missing are also associated with the phenomenon. Names
of the officers are being withheld pending notification of
their families.

So there you go. Dante and Jose, Mrs. Hayes' sister's neighbor's nephews, were the first to disappear into what would become one of the most puzzling and controversial natural events in recorded history.

*   *   *   *   *

But still several months earlier, still back in Washington…

I woke again in the hotel and once again started to move without thinking. First, I was in my suit. I was heading down the elevator. I was in the tunnels. By the time the fog broke and I finally let myself realize what was really going on, I was on another kamikaze mission in the lower halls of the White House.

This time around there would be no turning around. This time I had a purpose and no delusions about pulling it off. I'd fulfill my purpose or be arrested. I was tired of not doing anything. I was tired of being an observer. It was time I stopped assessing the world around me and became a participant in it. I was tired of having nothing to do.

Once out of the tunnel and into the hall, I found an empty office with a phone, dialed the operator and asked to be connected to the First Lady. Since it was an in-house line, the operator put me through to Colleen's assistant without question. I recognized Lisa Loenthou's voice. She clearly didn't recognize mine when I asked to speak to Mrs. Fisher.

"Who's calling please?" She asked with a touch of annoyance in her voice.

"Thomas Little."

"I'm sorry Mr. Little, Mrs. Fisher is not expecting your call and is busy at the moment. Can I tell her what this is regarding?"

"Ms. Loenthou, I have confidential information that I can share only with Mrs. Fisher." I figured using her name would add some legitimacy to my story.

"Mr. ... Little," she said unphased, "I don't know exactly what section you work in but almost everything we do here is confidential. I can assure you that I am cleared to pass along any information…"

I interrupted. "I have her test results."

"Test results?"

"Yes, I have the results of a medical test that Mrs. Fisher recently underwent and need to speak to her immediately."

"I am not aware of any tests…"

"Which reinforces my decision that Mrs. Fisher did not intend for me to pass on the results through a secretary."

"I am her personal Administrative Assistant…"

"Whatever. Are you going to put me though Ms. Loenthou or not?"

"Please hold."

After several minutes the line opened up.

"Hello?" I asked the silence.

"You're here again aren't you?" It was Colleen.

"Yes."

"Why?"

"I'm not sure."

"Where are you?"

"Two offices down from… where I came in."

"Stay there. I'm sending Lisa down to get you."

"Now it's my turn to ask why."

"Because I want to see my test results." The line went dead.

A minute later Lisa arrived and wordlessly reached out and unclipped my Lakeview ID badge and replaced it with an official visitor's pass. She then motioned me to follow and before you could say "security breech", I was standing in the private office of the First Lady.

Lisa excused herself, closing the door behind her.

I learned several things that day. I learned that all the telephone lines in the White House could be and probably were, monitored. I learned the coffee in the White House is not as good as you would expect it to be. I learned that the First Lady hated the title and the unrelenting spotlight that defined her life disgusted her more than it angered her. I learned she loved animals and that her favorite color was red and that her favorite vacation spot was a cabin near Howe Sound in British Columbia that had been in her family for years. I learned that it was not unusual for First Ladies in the past to discreetly see therapists.

I learned that she had time available and wanted to talk. I also learned that I enjoyed listening to her talk.

*   *   *   *   *

From that point on, as far as White House staff were concerned, I became the First Therapist. Although this was never actually announced or even spoken out loud by anyone who would know, the understanding of my role passed quickly, almost telepathically, through the entire executive staff. Everyone knowing and no one talking. It was just part of how it was.

Lisa gave me cash, which she thought was under the table payment for my services. Its real purpose was to allow me to get some decent clothes. If people were thinking I was her therapist, the least I could do was look like one. Only Colleen said it in a way that made me smile.

I asked if I should grow a goatee but she said I'd be too fashionable.

*   *   *   *   *

On my third visit I met the President for the first time.

He ignored me. He was perturbed that Colleen had been quoted as agreeing to the statement that raising taxes was "not necessarily a bad thing." He was afraid the Democrats and liberal media would run with that sound bite like "a mutt with a hot dog off the grill." And another thing, the dress she wore two nights ago at the state dinner for the Latin American Economic Summit Leaders, was "totally inappropriate".

For her part, Colleen pointed out the President of the United States could communicate with Burma but couldn't manage to have a decent discussion with his wife. If she'd seen him in the past four days maybe he could have helped pick out a dress that was more "appropriate" for Latin Americans.

And it all happened like I wasn't even there.

In the moments after the President left, Colleen of course apologized but said that she was glad that at least one person, whose job didn't depend on the President, had been able to see what was really happening. She said that she was tired of everyone expecting her life to be a fairy tale. She thought it was interesting that he was so arrogant that he had not even seemed to notice that I was in the room. I didn't find that interesting at all. I was used to it.

What I did find interesting was that all of us would like to think that the men in charge know what they were doing. That they were somehow above emotion. That men who captain torpedo boats have the ability to reason. That Governors and Prime Ministers will not lose their tempers. That doctors would know enough to exercise and that ministers would leave a note if they hit your car in a parking lot.

In an amazing number of cases all this may be true but our expectation of our leaders is perfection and perfection is a synonym for disappointment.

I learned that our relationship with Latin America was now strained, in the mind of the President, because the First Lady wore a dress that was "too pale". I tried not to be disappointed.

*   *   *   *   *

President Frank Fisher was many things in addition to a fashion critic. He had been born in Ohio, the "cradle of presidents", to a well-to-do family with a lineage that would make a show dog proud. He was a conservative Republican who had been elected by an overwhelming margin in what is widely agreed to have been the most negative Presidential race in history. President Fisher was a good looking man with perfect teeth, perfect posture and a perfect past. He regularly infuriated the liberal left by wearing a Ten Commandments pin on his lapel, with his sermonizing style and his frequent use of the word "Amen" during speeches. Depending on your political affiliation, he oozed either confidence or arrogance.

*   *   *   *   *

By the fourth time Colleen and I met we were no longer a source of gossip and had normalized into the white noise of the day to day operations of the White House. I still entered and exited through the tunnel. I suppose she could have issued me clearance to enter through the same entrance other employees used. I would guess that she didn't because she had issues with authority and that she received some sort of kick out of sneaking me in and out right under everyone's noses. This may have been an issue we could have addressed in therapy if we really had been doing therapy.

What we were really doing was simply talking. That and playing Scrabble. Therapy is a one-sided affair where both parties are working together for the benefit of one. Like a coin flip, our conversations had a "heads" and a "tail".

Colleen turned out to be a surprisingly good listener. She had a pearly hard exterior that was a perfectly crafted, protective mask. Once she cracked it off and stepped out, you realized that she was quite a different person. Like a butterfly. Yes, she was very much like a butterfly – beautiful and ready to fly.

When the conversation landed on her side of the coin, she told me everything. And I listened. At first, I don't think it was so much a matter of her trusting me. She knew that she could simply deny anything said. Given my past, my recent breaking and entering and my lack of accomplishment in general, her word would be accepted without question. I was a safe disposal of information.

Later, after this story broke and I was reluctantly famous for the first time, the question reporters and talk show hosts asked me the most was "What did you and the First Lady talk about?"

I would tell them that we talked about everyday kind of things, never about anything that had to do with government or national security. She clearly had an understanding and an interest in these topics however. She was, and still is, a keen political mind. That was simply just not what we talked about.

The reporters and the talk show hosts and their ratings also wanted to know if we ever talked about the Presidential sex life. I would laugh, shake my head and lie. "No, nothing like that" I would say. But we did after a while. And I guess I didn't really lie because according to Colleen, there wasn't any Presidential sex life to talk about. You see, the President hadn't had sex with the First Lady in the White House. Ever.

What a waste.

A real therapist could never have said that but that is exactly what I did say to her. I never mentioned *that* to the reporters and talk show hosts.

*   *   *   *   *

Somewhere between visit four and visit ten, I took the time to look up and read the official bio of the First Lady. I had been struck by her easy manner and her intelligence but I had no idea from where she had come. Her background was one of those facts that, most likely, most Americans knew well but that had somehow slipped by me. Not watching enough TV, I suppose.

I made up for past sins however, and read all I could find. Had I known at the beginning of this little odyssey what I learned from the official White House bio of Mrs. Colleen Fisher, I most likely would have made a even bigger ass out of myself and the events that I will soon share with you may have never happened in the manner in which they did. I may not even be writing what you are reading right now. But I didn't know then what I know now. So I am writing and you are reading. It's interesting the way things happen.

Colleen Fisher was born in Indianapolis, Indiana. Her father, Joseph Carson, was a middle school teacher and his father was a salesman in a hardware store. Joe was the first Carson to go to college and Colleen became the second. There was a difference however. Colleen entered college when she was just thirteen with a perfect SAT score.

As impressive as that was, it wasn't unexpected. She had learned to play the piano at age three and the violin at six. When her younger twin siblings, who were only a year younger than

Colleen, were building doll houses out of shoe boxes, she was doing crossword puzzles and quadratic equations.

She eventually graduated from Princeton with a Masters degree in mathematics at the ripe old age of seventeen and a half.

When I met this brilliant woman, she was wearing sweats, eating a McMuffin at McDonalds.

*   *   *   *   *

It wasn't until my tenth visit before things started to blow up. This explosion would eventually be much larger than when my little Seaview Mental Health had imploded on itself. That implosion thrust me into unemployment and a prescription for Prozac. In contrast, when my visits to the White House finally exploded, the resulting blast threw me clear past unemployment and into celebrity.

The night before what would become my last visit, I had called Norm's nursing home to see if he had made it back OK. A nurse who didn't sound as if she gave a damn, told me that Mr. Norman hadn't yet returned from his holiday. I asked her when she expected him back and she said she really didn't know and would have to be going, goodbye.

I wasn't overly concerned but between Marcus' bouts with paranoia and Norm's forgetfulness, there was potential for some interesting diversions from the expected. After allowing visions of log cabin hideouts to elope from my brain, I reminded myself that while Marcus was, at times, delusional, he was reasonably intelligent and could certainly handle Norm. And Norm… well Norm was Norm.

No sooner had this little overly parental episode played out in my head than came a knock on the hotel room door. I answered the door and my original question answered itself — Marcus walked back into the room and into the impending excitement. The irony was that he had come back because he and Norm were worried about me.

For each of us pompous enough to worry about someone else not being able to take care of themselves, there are two people worrying about us.

Marcus had taken Norm, as per Norm's request to his niece's house in Atlanta. She wasn't home at the time, so he left Norm on the doorstep. They both thought it would make a wonderful surprise.

Marcus was back.

I was having fun.

*   *   *   *   *

Like reading one of those advertisements on the hood of a pest control company truck, it all makes sense when you look at it in the rearview mirror. Marcus' primary assets were his brutal honesty and his not so subtle sense of humor. Unfortunately, his primary symptom was an unshakeable belief that government agents were following him. My decision to take him to meet Colleen in the White House, a place infested with scurrying Secret Service types, was not the best decision I have ever made.

I'd assumed that Marcus' life needed the same jump-start that mine did. I made the classic mistake of projecting my desires onto him. Marcus was fine the way he was.

So much for self-assessment.

*   *   *   *   *

Not only was Marcus fine the way he was but at this time, he was doing better than he had been in a while. His paranoia was almost completely under control and he was about to move out of my place and into a small two bedroom apartment with a roommate named Larry Litts. Larry was quiet and kept to himself. With the exception of an obsessive-compulsive cleaning habit, he may have been the perfect roommate. For Marcus, whose personal hygiene left a little to be desired, a little obsessive-compulsive cleaning around the apartment wasn't necessarily a bad thing.

*　　*　　*　　*　　*

So if I didn't think we were doing "therapy", what did I think was going on? In my mind it was pretty clear and I let the idea push its way right up front too, like a rabid fan at an eighties Stones concert. I had fallen under the spell of an intelligent, powerful and beautiful woman and I was breaking laws left and right, both legal and moral, to be with her for an hour or two each week.

What did she think we were doing? Did she think our meetings were therapy? If she did, it would have meant that I had compromised my ethics as a therapist and would have moved me up to the Triple Crown of low lifes – a legal, moral *and* ethical lawbreaker.

*　　*　　*　　*　　*

However misguided, my attempts to inject a little stimulus into the veins of Marcus' life was successful for the most part. He seemed excited about the prospect of meeting the First Lady. The day I brought him to the White House, he had dressed well and nodded politely to everyone we passed. Once we were in Colleen's office, he seemed excited and inquisitive.

Colleen clearly liked Marcus from the moment she met him. His life was a millennium away from hers. She grew up in middle America, her future offering a variety of roads all of which led to comfort and prosperity well beyond that of her parents. Marcus' choices for travel were fewer and led nowhere exotic. Despite their differences, Marcus and Colleen seemed to share a desire to understand the place the other had come from, and more importantly, they shared a nonjudgmental way of exploring that place.

Colleen asked Marcus if he'd ever done crack. He had but didn't like it.

Marcus asked Colleen if rich white women had a thing for black men. She didn't but knew of some that did.

And so on.

I'm not sure what the talk was among the White House staffers regarding the reason for Marcus being there. He only spoke one word in all the time he was there to anyone other than Colleen. Most likely, they believed I had brought him in for a second opinion.

"Oh my, Mrs. Fisher must be quite a difficult case."

After almost two hours with Colleen, I realized that Marcus and I had pushed past what was wise and should leave before our luck changed. In one of those miracles of synchronicity, as I was thinking about luck, the door burst open and the President strode in. Luck slipped by him unnoticed and left us for someone who deserved her.

"Really Colleen," he said, "This is getting out of hand. People are beginning to talk."

"To talk about what Frank?"

"This... your therapy. It doesn't look good at all. And now you've got two of them in here. It's one thing to look like you need a little support but this... this looks like you have problems. Serious problems."

"I don't have any problems Frank." She was totally calm.

"I know that but..." he stopped pacing and turned toward Colleen, confused. "Then why the therapy?"

"What therapy?" She was smiling now.

"What do you mean 'what therapy'? This therapy." He pointed accusingly to me. "The therapy that you've been undergoing for weeks now. I may seem like I don't care but I do Colleen. I notice. I run the country and make decisions that effect millions of people everyday but I notice."

"I'm sorry Frank, I'm not sure what you mean."

I sat there like a kid at his best friend's house when his parents break into an argument over the fact that she served brussel sprouts three times this week.

"My God Colleen, are you truly that naive? This is the God damn White House. You cannot possibly believe that you can bring a therapist in here twice a week and that I won't know about it. Everyone knows about it and I know more than everyone."

"Frank, I'd like you to meet Thomas Little and his friend Marcus." She said pointing to us with her palm up in much the same way she would introduce us if we were a couple of princes from some oil rich, third world country.

Out of habit I think, the President turned to us nodded his head and extended his hand.

Before I could move, Marcus reached out, firmly grabbed the President's hand, pulling him slightly off balance with the gusto of his handshake. As their eyes met, Marcus leaned forward and spoke softly.

"Bang."

*   *   *   *   *

Prior to that moment, I honestly had forgotten Marcus' past Presidential history. Had I remembered, for his sake, I never would have brought Marcus to the White House in the first place. He was harmless. It was one thing if I was found out, but even though he was harmless, if Marcus was found he'd be crucified as a lunatic who surely was out to kill the President.

As soon as I heard what Marcus had said, I stepped forward, grabbed the President's hand, shook it and explained that we really must be leaving. The presidential mouth stayed dropped open and his eyes stayed fixed on Marcus.

Colleen hadn't heard Marcus.

"These are my friends Frank, not my therapists. They are here because I asked them to come not because I need anyone to fix me."

The spell broken, the President turned toward the First Lady. "Your friends?" He asked.

"Yes, my friends." She said. "Now if you will excuse me, I'd like to say goodbye and show them out."

He looked at us and then back at her and then back at us. After a moment he turned around and walked out, closing the door behind him.

Colleen could not contain her pleasure in having confounded her husband.

"You two," She said with a smile "had better be leaving."

"You think?" Marcus replied.

She turned to me. "I guess our little adventure is over. If you come back, we're both in trouble."

It was true. The next time I showed my face, there would be a million questions. It was time for goodbye. My mind became a vacuum, sucking up any words that may have been combined into a meaningful description of what I felt, a heartfelt goodbye or even a clever parting comment. It was an important moment and, once again, I came up short.

"Goodbye Colleen." I said finally.

"Goodbye Tom." She leaned forward and kissed the air next to my face, gently touching her cheek to mine.

*   *   *   *   *

Marcus and I left Colleen's office, quickly making our way to the tunnel and back to my hotel room. I checked out and we were on the road for Florida within an hour of having skipped out of Colleen's door.

We stopped at the same hotel we'd stayed in on the way up and Marcus' old habit of looking out the front window for the FBI took on a whole new light.

President Fisher would ask questions and Colleen would provide elusive answers. He would get his people on it and eventually they'd find out that I had been staying across the street at the Washington. Through my credit card receipt, the trail would lead back to Florida and eventually back to me. During the long quiet miles on the drive home, I wondered what, if anything, they could actually charge me with other than befriending the First Lady. Marcus, on the other hand already had three strikes against him – he was a black, mentally ill man who had made a bad first impression. He would definitely suffer in some way if he got caught.

The thing Marcus had going for him was that he was difficult to track down. He moved often and didn't work so there just wasn't much to find.

Even riding the rest of the way back to Orlando with me was risky for Marcus. They could have cars out after us already. When I suggested to him that we take different routes home he refused. I did get him to promise though that once we made it back, he'd move. Maybe to Tampa or Jacksonville.

He said I was paranoid.

The interesting thing about the situation was that now I was the one worrying about being followed. Marcus handled it like he had his entire adult life. Pulling up and moving because the FBI was closing in was nothing new for him. He'd done it before and knew the routine. He even offered to help me disappear into the Florida Keys but I declined. Marcus was in his element and the ride home was, for him, the most fun he'd had in a while.

*   *   *   *   *

Once we arrived in Orlando, I bid Marcus goodbye and returned to my apartment and waited.

It didn't take long.

There were two wiry Secret Service types at my door asking questions within a day. They must have been bored because they went away quickly, which worried me more than it made me feel better. However, my problems were just beginning.

*   *   *   *   *

The White House is a big place filled with many, many people. Apparently, some of whom have a second job of leaking information to the press. Within two days my name was out. Shortly thereafter some editor decided there was a story and I was on my way to being famous… for the first time.

Corey Cohn was the first person to interview me. A reporter with a local alternative paper, Corey had much in common with Marcus. He wasn't black and he wasn't schizophrenic but both Corey and Marcus shared a deep seated belief that things were never as they seemed. The difference of course, was that Marcus' neurotransmitters had betrayed him, whereas Corey's mind functioned fine. He just chose to use only part of it.

Corey didn't call or have "his people" set up a time with "my people." Neither of us had "people". He simply knocked on my door and I let him in.

Corey would ask me questions like "So what was it like to have an affair with the First Lady?" or "Weren't you afraid the President would walk in on you?" A chunk of my brain wanted to be angry with Corey but I couldn't. He wanted a story so badly that he was making it up as he went along. I suppose there was something wrong with that behavior but at the time, I found him more sad than offensive.

Still, I couldn't stop myself from inflicting a little punishment in that way we all do when someone behaves in a manner which falls short of our standards. We all seem to know at birth that our job is to alter the behavior of everyone around us until it matches our own. What we don't learn until we're waiting in the express lane at the grocery store with a bottle of Zinfandel and a tube of hemorrhoid cream over the 10 item limit, is that it's also the job of everyone else around us to try to alter our behavior to match theirs. And so life goes, all of us crashing into each other like bumper cars, trying to alter each other's behaviors, with very few people going anywhere but in circles.

My behavior altering punishment for Corey was rather mild. I simply made sure that anything I said was non-controversial, even boring, but at the same time, I'd wink or nod my head to give him the impression that his version of our wild affair was right on the money. In terms I would have used when I had nothing better to do than to study this stuff – I made sure my *non-verbal communication was incongruent with my verbal message thereby raising the subject's anxiety level.*

The end result was Corey busting a gut because he was convinced he was on the verge of uncovering some great cover up. However, being a print reporter, he could only write what was said. And my quotes didn't say squat. I kept him going for three hours before he took his bumper car and drove away in a huff.

"Little, why are you such an ass?" He asked on his way out.

"I don't know." I said, "Maybe it's because I have this thing for the truth."

"The fact of the matter is, the facts don't really matter." he said, "People want to believe. They need to. Even an arrogant ass like you can't stop them."

*   *   *   *   *

I'm not sure how it all got out from there. It may have just foamed up from Corey Cohn's imagination. Someone read his fictional account of what happened, he told someone else, and she told someone else. It may have been someone on the

White House staff who couldn't resist telling their spouse over Tuna Helper that the President was in a huff because he thought the First Lady was doing her therapist. It could have been the President himself in some misguided effort to gain some public sympathy.

I know how it didn't get out. Neither Norm, Marcus nor myself ever mentioned a word to anyone about what went on, although this would have been hard to verify as far as Norm was concerned. I'm fairly confident however that even if Norm had told someone, they would have told him in a nice way that he had food on his face, and sent him shuffling on his way.

Regardless of how it got out, it came out like Liberace. After Corey's little interview, I was deluged with phone calls. Reporters knocked at my door at 4:30 in the morning. I unplugged my phone. Mrs. Hayes complained that the TV crews outside my apartment were tramping down her flower beds and that she had half a mind to call that action reporter on TV to complain and get something done about it like he did about that woman in Lakeland who found a condom in her package of adult diapers. I pointed out that it was unlikely that the action reporter would take on his own employer but she seemed unphased.

Within a couple days I realized that it was more difficult for me to get out of my garage apartment then it was for me to get into the White House.

The gist of what they were reporting was that I, Colleen's "private therapist", had been having a relationship with the First Lady and that because of our "affair", the presidential marriage was on the skids. At this point, it didn't appear that anyone knew about the tunnel or even Marcus and Norm for that matter. The fact that I actually had been a therapist gave the story an air of authenticity that was too much to pass up.

I tried calling Colleen at the White House but couldn't get through. If my life had become a circus of Barnum and Bailey proportions then her life must have been a living hell. On the other hand, life on a slide beneath the magnified eye of the public was something to which she was accustomed, and based on what I had seen, her relationship with the President had already been embalmed and buried. The fact that she was being falsely accused of having an affair however, really boiled my butt.

The obvious reason for my anger was that having an affair with her had been exactly what I would have wanted to happen. Of course now, on some subconscious level, I was feeling guilty for causing all this even though I didn't really have an affair anywhere other than in my fantasies. So because I felt guilty, I felt anger at the media, the press, my neighbors and anyone else who spread the gossip about the First Lady.

Sometimes it sucks to be able to assess things. Especially in those moments when you are able to do it to yourself.

ROAR

*   *   *   *   *

I had run out of food on the second day of the media siege outside my apartment and in my mind, was in serious danger of starving. I couldn't get out the door without being accosted. My car was pinned in by a mobile unit from Channel 3 which was in turn pinned in by a blue sedan and two reporters who I suspected were actually Secret Service. I made an attempt to slip out well after midnight but the second I hit the lawn, lights came on and the place erupted with people yelling so I retreated back to my apartment.

I called for pizza but when the pizza guy arrived another reporter had bribed him to let her deliver the pizza instead. When I opened the door and reached for the pizza, I got a microphone stuck in my face. I slammed the door, forgetting to grab the pizza first. Mrs. Hayes was apparently too upset about her flower beds to think about bringing me food and I'm pretty sure that she had taken her phone off the hook because I'd get nothing but busy signals when I called to check on her. An in depth search of my cabinets revealed a can of tomato paste, three envelopes of Kool Aid and a jar of olives of undetermined age. I ate the tomato paste with a spoon straight from the can, swallowed the Kool Aid without even mixing it with water and ate the olives without even thinking about the potential consequences of eating food that may have been in my cabinet since the week I moved in.

98

By the third day, my hopes that the story would die had just about disappeared. There were *more* trucks outside than the previous two days. The truck from MTV actually had a marquee sign on the side across which scrolled messages like "Come on Tom... We're on YOUR side." Or "I want my juicy gossip."

Lying there on the verge of starvation, two things became clear to me. First, I had to set the story straight. By not cooperating, I was lending credibility to the accusations that had to be hurting Colleen. The second thing I decided was that I was going to bust out before I cooperated. I was not going to surrender. I was going to escape and then arrange to tell the story on my own terms.

When I was young, my brother and I made a sport of climbing onto the roofs our of neighbor's houses. It had started with our own house but once that summit was conquered we moved on to more difficult "peaks". The game evolved quickly from a day game to one that we had to indulge in only late at night. We would sneak out our window and climb down the gutter and meet a couple of the neighbor kids at a predetermined rendezvous. Then our "team" would decide on an objective and set off to climb it. The goal was never to harm anything or scare anyone, we simply wanted to climb up onto each house, make our way quietly to the highest point and then get down – without getting caught.

Many of the houses were easy. The ones with old TV antennas were hardly a challenge at all. It was like walking up a ladder. Others had trees with limbs that spread out conveniently over part of the roof. We'd simply climb the tree and drop down on the roof.

One house however, Mr. and Mrs. Noble's, represented the Mount Everest of our neighborhood. It belonged to the wealthiest people on the block. The Nobles were an old retired couple who had lived there longer than any of us could remember. There was no antenna because they already had cable. There were no trees near the house and to make matters worse, it was a three story building located on the corner that could be seen clearly from all directions. It had been deemed unclimbable by Brett Fargo, our next door neighbor at the time.

My brother Matt and I were stubborn and refused to give in to defeat. One night, we took a rope and some thin clothesline, slipped out the window and made our way to the edge of the Noble's yard. Matt tied a G.I. Joe who was missing a leg to one end of the clothes line, swung it in circles, gaining velocity and let it fly upward onto and over the roof. After hiding for a few minutes to be sure that no one had woke up, we tied the clothes line to the thicker rope and ran to the back of the house. I grabbed the G.I. Joe and pulled the thicker rope up and over the roof. Matt grabbed the end in the front yard and I grabbed the end in the back yard then we both walked to the side of the house where the chimney was located. Matt was now standing at the base of the house with both ends of the rope. The top of the rope was hooked securely around the chimney.

We still had two problems. One, we had three stories to climb, which was a long way to fall. Two, the side of the house with the chimney also happened to be one of the two sides facing a road.

It didn't matter though. This was Everest. Matt climbed and pulled like I had never seen before. After he made it to the top, it was my turn. My muscles screamed and I scraped my knuckles on the brick so bad that they bled. But I kept climbing. A car passed and I froze, trying not to attract attention, then I climbed on. Finally, I was on the top. We stood for a moment on the chimney and looked down on the neighborhood. We could see our school five blocks away. I could see our house and almost all of the houses we had climbed.

On the way down, we both got rope burns on our palms, severe enough that we had to tell my mother what had happened. She poured hydrogen peroxide on our hands, spanked us and told us that if she caught either one of us on anyone's roof again that she'd call the police and turn us in herself for trespassing. Brett said it didn't count because we used a rope. None of that mattered to me though. We'd seen the neighborhood from a place that no one else had ever seen it.

*   *   *   *   *

My brother Matt has grown up to be an adult who believes in Atheism. He goes to Atheist meetings, writes in an Atheist newsletter and is currently in Nepal trying to teach the monks to believe in not believing.

He nearly died in a car accident when he was 19 and contrary to what you often read, he claims to have seen no light, had no out of the body experience, no sense of well being, no floating... nothing, just several days of unconsciousness only to wake up with several broken bones, a ruptured spleen and a lot of pain. As result of this experience, he is not a big fan of any organized religion or anything that even looks like an organized religion.

And he regularly sermonizes about it.

More importantly to this story, because he is living across the globe immersed in his work as atheistic missionary, I didn't invite him to my wedding. Given my current occupation, which you will learn more about shortly, I know beyond a shadow of a doubt that he wouldn't come even if I begged him.

That and the fact that I'm still pissed off for all the times he beat me up when we were kids.

*   *   *   *   *

On the third night of the siege outside of Mrs. Hayes' garage, I put on dark clothing just as I had when I was nine, added a pair of gloves and snuck out the window onto the roof of the garage. There was a tree that overhung the garage in the back. I climbed out on the limb and across to another limb that overhung the house behind Mrs. Hayes'. Given my lumpy physical condition at the time, it must have looked fairly comical. I dropped down onto the single story home, walked across the roof and let myself down to the ground out of sight of the crowd on the street. I slipped across several yards and I was free.

An operation that would have taken a matter of seconds when I was young, took me over twenty minutes.

My first order of business: obtaining two double burgers, a large order of fries and a chocolate milk shake.

My second order of business was to decide what to do about the circus outside my apartment.

Things had been difficult before but nothing like this. Mrs. Hayes was good about letting me slip one or two weeks on the rent now and then but now I was a month late and I was pretty sure she was working up the nerve to talk to me about it. The tires on my car were bald and would probably blow any day, which was a problem because if it caused an accident, I didn't have any insurance. And now I was being stalked by a story hungry mob.

Without knowing it, I ended up back at The Hideaway, found my usual stool near the end of the bar and ordered a beer. After an hour or so, Norm came in and claimed the stool next to mine.

"So you're famous now?" He said after the bartender brought him a beer.

"Looks that way."

"So what's your problem?"

"You ever been famous?"

"No."

"Then you have no clue." I had spoken with Norm once or twice since we'd returned from our adventure and talking with him now should have made me feel better. It probably would have if we had been talking about anything other than my current situation. Now I just wasn't in the mood.

After ten minutes of silence I was pretty sure I'd hurt his feelings so I tried to change the subject, "So, you were right about the tunnels."

"Yea, I was."

More silence.

"So," Norm said "How much money have you made being famous?"

"Just because you're famous doesn't mean you're rolling in the dough."

"Would if it were me." He said, "I think it may be me anyway. I could be famous. I was there."

"What are you talking about?"

"I was there. I was in the White House. If people knew that I'd be famous too."

"Oh no, Norm." I said turning to face him "You are not going to be telling people anything. No one knows about that tunnel. If people find out it'll put the clamps on Colleen's only link to freedom. And if they find out that's how I got in, the whole therapist story will fall apart and people really will believe that we were having some kind of a fling or something."

"I may be an old man but you will not be telling me what I can and can't do." He said "I think it's real noble that you're thinking of *Mrs.* Fisher and all but I have to think about me."

He drew out the word "Mrs." just a little long.

"And…" he continued, "My advice to you would be to do the same. You need to think about yourself here. *Mrs.* Fisher will be fine I'm sure."

He did it again.

I'd like to say that I argued with him. I'd like to say that I stuck to my principles and talked him out of it.

I can't say either of those things.

*   *   *   *   *

Let me bring you up to date regarding my wedding plans. It's now 3:00 a.m. and I'm still not sure what to do about it, Writing down problems was one of the things I always suggested to my clients. Now I'm writing and writing, wielding my pen like a baton in the hands of a manic conductor, cutting and thrusting, attempting to part the dastardly fog around me and make some sense of the music.

It's not working very well. Instead of clearing the fog, I'm just breaking things and cutting into things I'd rather not cut into.

Once I heard a famous comedian say that the best advice he ever received was to commit. Commit wholeheartedly to each and every joke you tell. If it bombs, people will at least applaud your commitment.

So now I am committing to my pen. In the end fog will lift and I'll see clearly. If not, at least you'll applaud my commitment to the joke.

*   *   *   *   *

Now... one of the things that I still need to cut open, another bag in need of unpacking, is the memory of the unfortunate death of Forbes Maxwell, my friend and author of ROAR, the Religion of Absolute Randomness.

After I escaped from my apartment, after I ate, after I drank eight beers and listened to the musings, described earlier, of one Norman McGee, after all this, I realized it was night again and I didn't have a place to stay.

Staying at Norm's nursing home was obviously out of the question. Returning to my multimedia infested apartment was also not a realistic option. I hadn't heard from Marcus in days and, unless I needed to know the address of an all night laundromat where I could crash, he would likely be of little help anyway. My list of options had been whittled down to one: Forbes Maxwell.

*   *   *   *   *

Forbes Maxwell had moved to a new house with statues and a dock along a spring fed lake. His early books were still racking up sales and he was finally reaping some modest benefits.

To be honest, as I made my way up the driveway, I felt a little guilty because I knew in several moments I would lie and tell him what a triumph I thought his latest work was when in reality, I had not even read his second or third book let alone "ROAR".

"Thomas!" Forbes proclaimed as I entered the room "How are you doing?"

"I'm OK."

"Yes you are." He walked through the motions of the old ritual.

"Your latest...what a triumph."

"Really? Do you really think so?"

"Absolutely. Your best to date."

Forbes was still in his robe and looked as if he had been that way all day.

"Oh, thank you. I have been so worried, it's such a departure from my normal work. I don't know what came over me. Now they want me to go on the most outrageous promotion tour. I'm not sure…" He paused for a moment, looking right at me. "So what have you been doing with yourself since our Seaview died?"

He didn't even wait for an answer.

After leading me silently back to his library, Forbes sat down on the sofa and stared at the floor. Across from him, sitting in a red velvet wing backed chair that looked as if it had been lifted straight from some Texas bordello, sat a smiling Karen Eli Windslow.

I had met Forbes' agent in person only once before. Her younger sister had been "Baker acted" which was Floridian for committed against her will to a psych facility, after attempting to cut her wrists. She was brought to Seaview by a sheriff's deputy with his gut hanging over his belt, several more chins than required hanging from his face and a cheap cigar hanging from the side of his mouth.

"She really meant it huh?" He said pointing to her bandaged arms as if she couldn't hear. He was referring to the fact that she had cut herself vertically, along the length of her arm rather than horizontally, across the wrists. While you could die either way, the former was considered more lethal since it was more difficult to treat quickly.

"Yea, she meant it." I responded not bothering to hide the irritation in my voice. "What she meant was that she needs help and no one was listening. Now be a good little policeman and go give someone a ticket."

I'd known it wasn't the most appropriate thing to say but I'd said it for Kelly Windslow, the 18 year old, black haired, tattooed, multi-pierced kid who sat shivering in front of me. She looked up and managed a thin smile as the deputy grumbled his way out of the room.

Kelly was Karen's younger sister. No sooner had I started my screening when Karen burst into the interview room and demanded that I release her sister. After my long winded explanation regarding the Florida Baker Act, its purpose to protect the rights of the mentally ill and the legal reality that only a psychiatrist could overturn an involuntary commitment, Karen Eli Windslow, once again demanded that I release her little sister, who, in Karen's mind, was not mentally ill and was simply pulling another one of her stunts to embarrass the family.

I started again, this time explaining how I was there to help Kelly and, to be totally honest, how I was currently breaking the law by even speaking to her without Kelly's consent and signature on a Release of Information Form. Karen Eli Windslow again demanded that I release her sister.

During this debate, Kelly stared blankly. When she looked at me in response to a question, it was as if she were looking through me. She looked as if whether she left with her sister or remained on a locked inpatient psychiatric ward mattered as much to her as whether she'd eaten or showered for the last three days.

It mattered to her as much as a broken leg on a flea on a pet dog's butt, It's not that Kelly didn't care, it was that she couldn't.

The difference between being depressed and being in the place Kelly was, is that when you are that far gone, you know that not only is there nothing you can do to help yourself but that it's hopeless to even think that anyone has any chance what-so-ever to make any difference what-so-ever. Kelly's behavior was understandable to me, being the assessor of things that I was, Karen Eli Windslow's behavior however, sent gobs of neurotransmitters flying between the synapses of the information gathering antenna of my brain.

No, going home with her older sister did not seem to be a good option for Kelly.

I know, I know, that seems like a pretty quick conclusion to draw from a woman who's little sister was about to be locked away in a psych ward and I have no real defense except to say that I was a professional. So kids, don't try this at home.

Karen is now my agent and interestingly, the name of my dog but I'll get to that later.

Since that time, so long ago, I have become famous for a second time for an entirely different reason and Karen Eli Windslow and I have made a great deal of money together.

A great deal of money.

*   *   *   *   *

But back then, in Forbes living room, it was clear that I had interrupted something.

Karen's smile was a smile that required a great deal of effort. The kind of effort that was usually reserved for individuals who represented more commas and zeros in their bank statements than she felt I did at the time. She quickly let the smile fall, shot Forbes a "get rid of him" look and walked to the window. She looked outside, the smoke from her cigarette trying to escape her lips by climbing up the glass.

"Forbes, I'll get right to the point," I said, "I need your help."

"What do you need old friend?"

That was nice to hear. Forbes and I had worked together for years but I always thought I was stretching the definition of "friend" when I used the word with him. I was never really sure if our relationship had moved up to the friend box but now he looked as if he needed one and I knew I certainly did, so I pressed forward.

"I need a place to stay. Just for a couple of nights until I can go back to my apartment."

"What's wrong with your apartment?"

"It's a media circus. There are TV, radio and newspaper people all over the place."

At the sound of the word "media", Karen extinguished her half smoked cigarette, returned to the chair and put some second effort into her smile.

"Why are the media outside your apartment?" She asked.

"Haven't you read the papers?" I asked.

"I was interrupted after the Style section and didn't get to the Local section."

"It was on the front page." I said.

"I missed that section too."

"Tom, what happened?" Forbes asked. "Is it something you did? Are you in trouble?"

I explained to them what had transpired over the past several weeks and asked if I could stay for the next couple of days.

"I'm sorry Tom but Karen is staying in the guest room and…" Forbes started.

"Forbes, its OK." Karen interrupted, her smile now working at full strength. "I don't mind sharing your hospitality with Tom if you are willing to lend him a hand."

I was offered the couch.

They say things always happen in threes. Three important things would happen that night. First, Forbes died. Second, Karen Eli Windslow was about to offer me my second bout of fame. And the third was that I stayed up the entire night reading Forbes' book.

And his book confirmed my idea that things only happen in threes if that is where you stop counting.

*   *   *   *   *

The reason Karen was staying at Forbes house was to get Forbes to do a book tour, touting his ROAR as the "religion for a new century." The fact that Forbes' personality was the antithesis of the circus barker mentality required for such a tour reflected the desperation into which Karen was slipping. Sales of ROAR were leveling off and in the pond that is the world of publishing, stagnated sales were surrounded by the rotting corpses of authors and agents who once walked on water. Karen and Forbes had just started skipping across the puddle of decent sales and Karen was determined to make it all the way to the ocean.

The people buying Forbes' book were looking to be told once again how wonderful they were. They were the fractured, the insecure. Instead of reassurance they found something else and they didn't understand it. I'm not sure that Karen really understands it even today, but then, she was reading the times and felt that something in Forbes book might be the lucky ping pong ball that could pop to the top of the literary lottery.

Karen had come to get something from Forbes and I had come to get something from Forbes. Forbes was sitting in between us with his head in his hands, rocking slightly from side to side. He did not like Karen's plan and had no desire to travel the country like some carny hawking a chance to see a freak show. Forbes was Greta Garbo with less hair. He functioned better alone and having a single house guest put him in a social overload red zone. Having two put him over the edge.

"I have to go to the bathroom." Forbes said finally, heading for what he probably thought of as his last sanctuary.

Although he was hardly involved in it, once Forbes left the room the conversation left with him. Karen and I were left staring around the room trying to find something to look at other than each other.

After a couple of minutes we heard the bath water start to run. It stopped. Silence for a minute, and then two claps, loud music, a membrane popping wail, a crash, a scream and more silence.

We ran into the bathroom to see what was going on.

*   *   *   *   *

I'll bet there have been lots of people whose last words were "I have to go to the bathroom."

*   *   *   *   *

"Jesus Christ." Karen spoke in a whisper.

Forbes was in his bathtub. Dead.

I turned down the TV and carefully unplugged the electric Shitsu massager that was in the tub with him. Glancing around the room, it was immediately clear what had happened that had caused Forbes to join the honor roll of the rich and famous who have bought it in the bathroom.

Forbes had drawn himself a bath. Gotten in the tub. Clapped his hands to turn on the TV. The TV came on suddenly startling the cat that jumped off the counter knocking the massager into the tub, electrocuting Forbes.

"Jesus Christ." Karen said again.

"I know. Are you alright?" I asked.

"Jesus Christ." She said this time looking at me. "I know. He…"

"Not him. You."

"What?"

"You." She said with what might be considered a smile. "You've got the job."

"What in the hell are you talking about?"

116

"Forbes is dead. That leaves a position open. People know you. You are going to be the Christ of the Religion of Randomness, The Buddha of ROAR."

*   *   *   *   *

Good marketing is about creating a buzz. Creating a buzz is about secrecy. That and controlling the flow of information.

The first thing Karen Eli Windslow did was to remove the Clapper from the TV set.

"What are you doing that for?"

"Because he committed suicide."

"He what?"

"A religious martyr would not die because his pussy cat knocked a cheap Japanese appliance in the tub with him. A martyr would die nobly and what is more noble that suicide? And he sure as hell wouldn't be using a Clapper." She stuffed the Clapper into her purse and reached into the tub with both hands and splashed water all over me. She then went to the phone and called 911.

When the police arrived I listened as she explained how Forbes must have purchased the massager for the sole purpose of taking his own life and cleansing his soul of this world.

I slowed down and watched like I was a commuter tapping the brakes to get a glimpse of a head on collision.

"...and came around the corner and found Mr. Little holding the body in his arms, clearly distraught over the loss of his friend." Karen was talking to the detective. "It was... so touching." The police all nodded their heads sympathetically.

Then one of them turned his head and looked at me. "Hey, aren't you the guy that banged the First Lady?"

*   *   *   *   *

I feel I need to explain my actions during this time. Why it matters, I've decided, probably has something to do with the fact that I saw myself as an unemployed, overweight male, of mediocre intelligence who contributed very little to the pile of accomplishments produced by human existence. So it is important that you understand that what you are about to hear was not the decision of a greedy, self serving assessor of men but rather the misguided decision of a man who was at the end of his rope.

Really.

I swear.

*   *   *   *   *

Karen Eli Windslow had hit the nail on the head and drove it right into my pocketbook. Any subconscious seeds that Norm may have planted in my brain about parlaying my fame into some sort of profit were going to die before anyone ever even noticed them. Nobody was going to stay interested in the therapist of the First Lady for very long. There were lesbians in pet custody battles, parents whose kids actually did homework, coworkers who were intolerable to work with due to the disgusting noises they made with their noses and migrant workers who could recite the Gettysburg Address. All these people were, deservingly so, more interesting than me. My main vein, once I punctured it, would run dry very, very quickly. My gold rush had ended before I knew enough to even know it was potentially there.

And here was Karen slithering into my life with the apple that would solve my financial troubles and make me famous for real to boot.

*   *   *   *   *

The minute the police left, she grabbed my hand and led me into the living room.

"Are you OK?" she asked.

"Yeah, I think so." I said, "What about you?"

"I don't know. I'm pretty shaken up." She said it so smoothly that it sent my cerebral bacon to sizzling. I had the feeling even then that there wasn't much that could actually shake this woman.

"It is such a shame." She went on, "He was on the verge of truly making a difference."

"Yea, I think he touched more and more people with each one of his books."

"Ha!" It blurted out of her mouth with so much force that she must have startled herself but she recovered quickly. "No. No. No... you don't understand. You haven't really read his last book have you?"

"Well... I was meaning..."

"It is different. He was beginning something special. That's why I was here tonight. Forbes and I were planning on the proper way to unleash the power of "ROAR" on the world."

Somehow, although I am fairly sure I was staring at her the entire time, she was now magically close enough that I could feel her breath blowing softly across my cheek.

"This book," she was almost whispering "was going to change the world. And… make Forbes a very, very rich man." She abruptly stood and turned away reaching for her coat. "But I guess that's all in the past now."

I would like to portray myself to you now as having been naive enough not to have realized what was happening. I even tried to be naive. I acted naive. I'm sure I looked naive. Here and now however, telling you this, I know that I knew then, exactly what Karen Eli Windslow had in mind. I didn't stumble into it nor was I misled by the soft breathing serpent that she so clearly was.

Her words were so predictable that I could have written her script.

"…if only he hadn't of died…if only there were someone to pick up his torch…he could become the.."

"Martyr?" I finished her sentence.

"Exactly!."

It is like playing "Scissors, Paper, Rock." You try to guess what your opponent will do and then counter with a move that will defeat his move. Then you think about it a second longer and realize that that is exactly what he expects you to do so you have to think a level deeper to out fox him. I'm not sure if I was a level ahead of Karen or if she was actually playing a level deeper than me. It didn't matter. She needed me for something. Women like her don't look at men like me with looks like that.

Somehow I played into her scheme to make a lot of cash off of Forbes' new book and somehow him dying had just sweetened the pot rather than spoiling the stew.

I decided it was time I read the book.

*　　　*　　　*　　　*　　　*

Which is the more likely event - a) that the flip of a coin will come up heads or b) that two children in a class of 25 first graders would have the same birthday? If you were one of the approximately 1,209,000 people world wide who would purchase Forbes' book after Karen Eli Windslow and I took it over, or one of the 157,000 who would purchase it on tape, or one of the 308,000 who would purchase the multimedia software version or one of the countless who, much to the angst of Karen, downloaded portions illegally on the Internet, you would know that it is more likely that the first graders would be blowing out candles together than you winning a coin toss.

Every great religion deserves a great language. In "ROAR", Forbes often chose to speak to his flock in the universal language of mathematics. If you, being one of the unconverted, are confused, let me explain. First, I'll handle the easy part.

In a coin toss there are two options which are equally likely to occur (discounting the infinitesimally small chance that the coin could land on its edge which according to Forbes is to be expected but I'll save that for the advanced lesson later.) It could be "heads" or it could be "tails". 50/50. 50% chance of it being heads. Simple.

However, once our biological brain baggage starts traveling, thinking about the 25 screaming first grade children, and then throws in 365 days and bounces those numbers around and comes up with something like... well... we're not quite sure but it has to be less likely than a 50/50 chance. Well, it isn't. And it isn't that complex. This is how I would later paraphrase page 125 of the Book of Probabilities in "The Religion of Randomness":

"Tyler is the first child in class. Front row, by the door. His birthday is May 5th. Looking around the room, it's easy for us to see that there are 24 yelling, jumping chances for someone to have the same birthday as Ty. Jennifer sits next to Ty. He cheats off her but that's OK because he'll likely become a surgeon and save children's lives before they even leave the womb. Jennifer's birthday could be the same as Tyler's in which case we already have a winner but most likely it is not. Jennifer has 23 other kids who may share her birthday though. Michelle, sitting next to Jennifer has 22. Joshua K. has 21 and so on. Now if we add up Ty's chances with Jennifer's chances with everyone else's chances... 24(Ty) + 23(Jennifer) + 22(Michelle) + 21(Joshua K.) + 20(Binky) + 19(Joseph) + 18(Lori) + 17(Brett) + 16(Marty) + 15(Dan) + 14(Ricky) + 13(Charles) + 12(Joshua S.) + 11(Samantha) + 10(Cathy) + 9(Tina) + 8(Falicia) + 7(Alan) + 6(Pedro) + 5(Kimberly) + 4(Sandy) + 3(Walter) + 2(Chris) + Delbert's one lousy chance and we get 300 chances out of 365 possibilities that would result in a joint birthday party. That's an 82% chance. It is this way because it is this way."

Many of us now know the facts but will refuse to believe. We'll believe that bug eyed creatures from outer space, somehow broke all laws of physics and made it across light-years of space only to stop by and let some farmer in Iowa videotape them for some TV news magazine. We'll believe in Bigfoot, the Loch Ness monster, astrology, tarot cards, lucky charms, and Oprah Winfrey. We flock to some oil spill on the bottom of a garage in a Dallas suburb and believe we are seeing Elvis's face because of some divine intervention. We believe we can win in Vegas and swear we always do. (Yet never question how they are able to build those sprawling neon infested casinos) We pray to long dead saints to help us find our lost keys.

If we grouped together by birth date the 1,209,000 people who bought Forbes' book, on any given day we'd have 3300 birthday girls and boys signing each other's cards.

*   *   *   *   *

Now is as good a time as any to share with you some interesting facts about Karen Eli Windslow and Colleen Fisher. Similarities which, on the surface, seem minor but when taken together seem amazing. Similar to the Kennedy – Lincoln coincidences you've probably read about in some magazine in some waiting room while waiting to get your teeth drilled.

Meeting the two women, your first impression would be that two females could not be further apart. Both are attractive, intelligent and articulate but that is where the similarities seem to abruptly end. Karen talks. Colleen listens. Karen knows. Colleen learns. Karen calculates how she can use others. Colleen considers how others can use her. And so on.

But there are some interesting similarities:

- Both play piano

- Both were brought up Catholic

- Both are left handed

- Both once had and have overcome a drug problem

- Both have fathers named Joseph

- Both were born in middle America to middle class parents

- Both had a deaf sibling and know sign language

- Although they never met, both lived within a block of each other in San Francisco for over a year, where they had both gone to "disappear" and re-invent themselves.

On the other hand, another difference was that where Colleen was on the verge of another reinvention, Karen was just turning up the volume on who she had become.

*   *   *   *   *

Whatever her faults, when it came to start-up religions, Karen Eli Windslow was the woman for the job. First, she made me give up cigarettes - no smoking prophets in this order. Then the personal trainer – I was to lose 30 pounds. The professional shopper was unnecessary because Karen handpicked my clothes.

Karen had a very specific look in mind and I could tell by what she didn't say that it was going to take some work to fit me into it. I did however, have my bright sides. People already knew my face so there was already some brand recognition. Also, although Karen's ideal ROAR messenger would look sharp and smart, he also couldn't be a pretty boy. And not being a pretty boy was something I was good at.

I have to admit that despite being uncomfortable during hours of snipping, measuring, shaving, fashioning, fitting, manicuring, trimming and buffing, when she was done with me, I felt and looked good. I would have been the first to deny it but we all look at the man in the expensive suit. The man in the khakis slides from our memories instantaneously unless he's missing an arm or drooling or talking to himself. The only khaki men we remember are those who we first knew in expensive suits. Now we think they are cool because they are casual - yet another scissors-paper-rock, level thing.

Marcus once described for me what it was like to be the target of prejudice. He said he could live with being called a "nigger" or with someone in a pickup with a rebel flag flipping him off for no reason whatsoever. They were just jerks who were in the back of the line when brains were being passed out. What was hard for Marcus to deal with were the subtleties. He said it was as if a thin layer of gauze had been thrown over the world. It filtered and separated everything, always. It takes years to even realize that it is there and the ultimate disappointment is the realization that you will never know what the world looks like without the gauze.

As I walked down the street in my new suit, people looked at me differently. I received more disrespect from some but more respect from most. Better service. More smiles. More women noticed me. My peacock feathers had never shown so bright. Despite the magazine articles that preach it's a man's sensitivity, personality and intelligence that women are attracted to, you can't see sensitivity, personality or intelligence. You can see a thousand-dollar suit. Unlike with Marcus, my gauze could be removed and Karen ripped it away like a breeze down Fifth Avenue. I realized that the gauze worked both ways, not only had it effected the way the world saw me but it effected the way I saw myself. In my suit, I could accomplish things. I straightened my back, lifted my chin, smiled more. These things no doubt contributed to the way others saw me as well and in a spiraling anti toilet flush sort of way, lead exactly to the place where Karen had intended me to go.

Corey Cohn had made me famous once. Now I was ready to be famous again but this time in a big way.

*   *   *   *   *

To the surprise of neither of us, Forbes' dying was one of the things that eventually would send ROAR over the top. Karen Eli Windslow could not have planned it better although it truly happened by chance. It seems the staying power of a dead prophet far outlasts that of a living breathing, tithe collecting one. Just ask Elvis. Actually, there were *several* things that helped rocket the book into the thin atmosphere of blockbuster bestsellers.

Forbes passing aside, the other thing that virtually assured that ROAR would float to the heights of culthood was that the book had been published with a page missing.

These two events, dying and losing a page, injected ROAR with the element of open interpretation. It was fairly esoteric to begin with but now it virtually oozed the stuff. What had he meant? What was the significance of Π in chapter three? Once it took off, the book caused these kinds of questions to be asked by teenagers grinding down the library steps, by women in hair nets shopping for organically grown vegetables, and by men drinking hard liquor in bars with walls covered with old black and white pictures of baseball heroes. They argued. They argued because Forbes' vision fit the template of hundreds of perfect arguments that came before it. Who was the best Beatle? Did Adam have an Adam's apple? Could Buddha rub his own belly for luck?

The missing page became a vacuum that sucked up opinions like a tornado imploding a barn, the opinions flew pretty much everywhere but after the dust cleared, the book was always left standing there.

Sixty-six. That was the missing page. The fact that it was only two digits and fell in the second chapter did nothing to stop the inevitable comparisons to the more famous "666".

Ironically, the least often accepted reason that page 66 was missing in a book called "The Religion of Absolute Randomness" was the real explanation - that it was a random accident.

What are the odds of that?

*   *   *   *   *

In the late sixties, a group of teenagers formed a organization called TMTSW (Teens Meditating Together to Stop the War – pronounced "Teemtswa") in Lankey, South Carolina. They began nightly meditation in hopes of inducing the end of the Vietnam war. They wore their hair long, beads and flowers and tossed about words like "love", "peace" and "groovy", yet the group did not prescribe to the open sexuality or drugs that defined that free spirited era. They were a focused group where "purity" was required to "advance to the level of influence". After meditating daily for weeks and then months the teens rejoiced when the war finally ended for America. They took out a full-page ad in the Lankey Keyhole, the local paper, to make sure their accomplishment did not go unnoticed. The teens stated "We often felt like giving up but now that we've ended the war, it's all worth it. Someday my children will appreciate what we've accomplished here."

I just looked into the archives of the Lankey Keyhole. Apparently, after the members of Timtsiwa became adults, they lost their amazing power to stop wars. Either that or they didn't feel the Persian Gulf war, Afghanistan and Iraq weren't worth the effort.

*　　*　　*　　*　　*

I am the one who is about no show at his own wedding. I am the one who bit willingly into the fruit of Karen Eli Windslow's apple. And now that you know me as a man who could do such things, I feel I can admit that, back in the beginning of this story, I had not really wanted to go Washington. The reason I didn't want to go was not that I doubted the existence of Norm's tunnels. Even sans tunnels, it sounded like a wonderful adventure - cherry blossoms, mindlessly wondering the halls of the Smithsonian, oh, the capital in the springtime. No, I would not have been upset at all if we never found even a foot of crawl space. The real reason for my reluctance was that, although I was an unemployed , overweight barstool warmer, I was concerned about what damage my precious image may incur by spending so much time with a semi-senile old fart (Norm's words) and a crazy black man.

As any good cognitive therapist worth her preferred provider status could tell you, our feelings are not a direct result of events that happen to us, but rather are a result of our underlying beliefs regarding the causes and potential results of those events. My feeling embarrassed had little to do with the behaviors of Marcus and Norm and a lot to do with several erroneous underlying beliefs I had stored in my brain like antiquated blue laws filed away in dust covered boxes. For example, the belief in the existence of people who could see past the gauze and even *notice* my image and, assuming there were such people, which there weren't, the belief that being a known companion of Norm and Marcus would be able soil a reputation that was already stained beyond the help of the most touted industrial strength detergent. In the less myopic vision of hindsight, me being embarrassed was akin to my father worrying about the wax job on the weed encased skeleton of the Stanc Standard that had sat silently up on crumbling concrete blocks in my backyard for nearly my entire childhood.

Up to this point, you may have obtained the impression that I am a foolish but well meaning screw up. That opinion might be partially correct. You may forgive my cruel prejudices regarding my friends as a result of a difficult childhood, a receding hairline, the loss of my job, etcetera, etcetera, etcetera. You may be right. I hope so. Maybe its just as case of pre-non-wedding jitters but right now, I am not so sure.

*　　　*　　　*　　　*　　　*

In my first week as Rajah of ROAR, I addressed a small crowd at Read and Write Bookstore. I met with the Winter Park Garden Club. By the end of the month, I had met with the Central Florida Motorcycle Enthusiasts Club, the Middlebrook High School PTA and the Orlando chapter of the Florida Association of Retired Persons. I was interviewed by the Orlando Weekly and met with the Rollins College Student Association. Over the next weekend, I traveled to Tampa and on Sunday to Miami where I did 4 additional book signings (signing a book I didn't even write). I addressed the Supporters of Our Public Library, the Florida chapter of the NAACP, the Windermere Little League organizational meeting, the Southeastern Gay and Lesbian Celebration of Freedom Parade, and Central Florida annual meeting of the National Rifle Association.

I was on my way.

*　　　*　　　*　　　*　　　*

In my early youth, before we moved to the suburbs, we lived in a house on the southwest corner at an intersection of two country roads. Every other corner of our intersection had a cornfield on it. Our property was an island washed in tides of corn. The main building started out as a small, traditional colonial home but after various additions, add-ons and expansions, it took on a Frankenstein like appearance. Some rooms dropped down several inches and, between rooms, there were several unnecessary doorways blocked by furniture and leading no where.

My father, for the record, did not add any of the additions to our house. The man who owned the surrounding fields rented the house, the lot and the old chicken coop in the back, to my father. I never met the man but he was an asshole. My father used to say that all the time.

My father didn't even like the country.

I did.

I used to sit sometimes on the swing on our porch and watch the cars barrel down the road toward the stop sign on our corner. They almost always stopped. This amazed me then and still amazes me now. No one was around for miles and they would stop. Sometimes I would think this was a good thing, representing a world full of law-abiding citizens who were good to the core. Sometimes I would think it was a bad thing, a demonstration of the boring, sheep like ways of adulthood.

Back then, as a child with a bottle of Chocola on the swing on the porch, I decided that it was a "bood" thing - half bad, half good. I really liked "gad" better but that had been taken.

In the books I would read at school, people would say things like "Eek Gad!" or "Jumpin Jehosaphat!" or "Holy Cow!".

While I never did figure out who Jehosaphat was or why he jumped, I became comfortable early on with a dichotomous view of things, with them being right and wrong or good and bad at the same time... or being even nothing at all.

$$* \quad * \quad * \quad * \quad *$$

I don't want you to think that I slid into the Ayatollah of Absolute Randomness role like fingertips into holy water. The truth is, I wasn't really buying what the book was selling at first.

The old "human eye argument", among other things, was still throwing me for a loop. How could this world with it's intricate ecology, something so complex, intricate, smooth, useful and beautiful have fallen together by chance? How could something as complicated, delicate and efficient as the human eye randomly evolve?

I was teetering and tottering between the "art must have an artist" argument that presented itself as I examined my eyeballs in the mirror and the hard cold math that was the foundation of Forbes' logic. Then something happened that heed me hard and hawed me cleanly onto one side of the sofa.

After my White House affairs went public, Norm made good on his promise to cash in on the moment and came out and told anyone who would listen about his role in our little adventure. While I had shot my initial wad of fame on the incident, there was still a little spotlight left for Norm. Not a whole lot of people listened but he did managed to parlay his story into more than his share of his fifteen minutes of fame.

A local radio station semi-adopted him, incorporating a daily call from Norm to their morning radio show. The bit was always the same basic format – A DJ with a precarious grasp on the English language would ask Norm a question about current events. Norm wouldn't know the answer so he would make something up. The ignoramuses would howl with delight at Norm's ignorance.

The first few times I heard it the bit made me angry. I'm not sure if Norm knew they were laughing at him rather than with him but Norm kept calling so he must have been getting something out of it. You could say a lot of things about Norm but one thing was for sure, Norm never did anything he didn't want to do.

*   *   *   *   *

I was on the radio as well… but not because I wanted to be.

The first time I was asked to go one the air was for a short interview on local public radio. Karen wasn't sure I could handle an interview so she arranged for me to give a speech in Branson Park in downtown Orlando. She packed the park with students from the University of Central Florida who she hand picked, coached and paid. She gave National Public Radio the exclusive rights to cover and broadcast the speech. She hired a group of top ad industry types to write the speech and then rejected what they came up with. She then wrote a short soliloquy herself that would ring over and over again like a bad song in a car commercial.

I threw them both out and just rambled until I ran out of words. I lasted about as along as I remember sex lasting. Which wasn't long.

*   *   *   *   *

My Branson Park speech in its entirety:

" *The patterns of our experience may turn out to be no more than ripples on a much bigger wave.*

"*There are boys, oblivious to Ruth and DiMaggio, chattering on a little league benches, arguing vehemently that the Yankees suck and have always sucked. There are old church going men who maintain that Germans and Japanese are kin to the devil. There were blacksmiths and hand maids in ancient Greece who engaged in flirtatious exchanges regarding the powers of Zeus and Athena.*

"There's a man in India who bows respectfully at the passing of a sacred cow and there's a boy in Detroit who slaps circular slabs of raw meat on a grill and serves them just the way the customer believes they should be.

"Forbes did not ask us to stop believing. He has never even suggested that your belief, or your belief, or my beliefs are any less valid than his. In fact, in the entire collection of Books, which make up the Religion of Absolute Randomness, he never states exactly what his beliefs are.

"What he does say is that we should continually question our view point.

"Close your eyes. All of you. Close your eyes and picture yourself as if you were floating somewhere near the ceiling, looking down at yourself. Look at the room that surrounds you. Look at what is important to you in that room.

"Now picture yourself pulling away, higher, through the ceiling, through the roof. You're now looking down on the neighborhood full of children playing in yards, dreaming of the future. Looking down on cars driven by business people worrying about proposals, projects and budgets. You see one teenage girl concerned she is pregnant, convinced her world is crumbling around her, and another heading toward her mailbox, where a letter awaits stating that she has been accepted into the college she'd never thought would even respond.

"Now go higher, above your city and it's crime, parks, gridlock and growth. Go above its skyscrapers, dealers, sorrows and hopes.

"Go higher still, above your country, continent and our planet.

"Now you must concentrate and allow yourself past your usual view. Looking down on the world, the solar system and the universe, let yourself float above time. Envision histories about which you've read and futures of which you've never dreamed.

"If you can picture this place, above the universe and time and picture for a moment, your arms fruitlessly trying to wrap around it. If you can then stop, drop your arms and simply let things be. If you can do this, then you will have felt the wave and will understand the Religion of Absolute Randomness."

That was my speech and at the time, I thought it was a load of crap.

*　　　*　　　*　　　*　　　*

The first time that I was supposed to be on TV was only slightly less successful than my radio speech. I was scheduled to be interviewed as part of the local Live Action Report at Noon on Channel 4. In the end, I was bumped for an investigative piece on abuse in nursing homes. I was sitting in a plastic chair eating a vending machine pastry and drinking stale coffee watching the news on a TV screen mounted near the ceiling in the employee cafeteria. I was bored. No one bothered to come tell me I was bumped until the broadcast was five minutes from being over. I stayed to watch the end of the broadcast because I didn't know what to say to allow me to excuse myself without embarrassing myself.

One of the homes featured in the piece that I got bumped for was the Golden Age Retirement Village. The Golden Age Retirement Village also happened to be the home Norm escaped from each night for his draft down at the Hideaway. Investigative reporter Lawrence Ledbetter acted sufficiently outraged in an effort to "get to the bottom of this so called care facility" but the sound was so low that I really couldn't tell if he ever actually made it to the bottom or not.

I remember Norm talking about it. He liked it. At that time however, he'd never needed a sponge bath.

*   *   *   *   *

Karen thought that modern day America might have a hard time relating to a religious icon who was single and had never been married. She said if Christ were alive today the media would "paint him gay and eat him alive." I asked her "So what if he was?" and to her credit she blew me off saying that question was even more irrelevant than it was irreverent and that we needed to focus and come up with something to soften my image enough to sell our message. So she focused and I softened.

140

As a general rule, Karen's thoughts revolved around money. She couldn't buy me a wife, although I'm sure she considered it at some length.

After a few weeks of thought, Karen bought me a dog.

She named her "Karen".

The first time I tried to pet her, she bit me. In time however, we came to an understanding and I have to say, I noticed that almost every picture of me in the major magazines included my dog. It was a brilliant move and I actually have learned to like the mutt.

At that time, Karen the Person was beginning to grow on me as well. "ROAR" was selling like no book had ever sold before. And 2% of a lot is a lot. As Karen pointed out, preaching is simply marketing a product that costs nothing. A product you can't see, feel or hear and has no warranty what-so-ever.

*   *   *   *   *

Speeches, meetings, coaching, make-overs, underlings, planning meetings, procedures, rulings, dogma, pronouncements, picking official colors, clothing and shoes. Interviewing, hiring, writing, filming, shaking hands, holding babies, waving, parading, walking, knocking, smiling, explaining, responding, flow charting, budgeting, image consulting. Singing, chanting, clapping and hiding at moments from the press. Second editions, Reader's Digest versions, children's versions, Braille versions and multiple translations. Gatherings in parks, in tea rooms, steam rooms and stadiums. Newspapers, newsletters, flyers pamphlets, sound bites, talk shows and guest appearances. Protests, supporters, believers and caffeine. And more caffeine.

And then I was famous.

Time bent in ways that would make a circus performer jealous and Einstein proud.

We hadn't yet considered curve balls of time (or knuckleballs or sinkers for that matter) but ROAR marched on like a sober man at a sobriety check – straight ahead. So let's, like nearly all of Forbes' faithful, march faithfully forward because it's the path of least resistance and more importantly, that's where the rest of this story lies.

*   *   *   *   *

Now that I was famous AND rich, I called Big Bob Wyatt's Stanc dealership in Ann Arbor, Michigan and located the owners of the ten known remaining 1995 Stanc c.12 Excelsiors. I called Dr. Donald Menkie, the first name on the list, offered him $500,000 and sent my people to go pick it up.

My Stanc c.12, like all twelve others ever made, was painted "Executive Grey" prior to being pushed out the door and sent on its way in the world to become rich and famous like me. The day it arrived, I had it painted metallic blue, added neon green under lighting and the bullet proof glass. I didn't like metallic blue or neon green. I figured if I could make my Stanc the ugliest, maybe it would become the most valuable. There was a reason Karen Eli Windslow was making all the decisions.

*   *   *   *   *

We are now several notches nearer my impending non-wedding. I am still here, sitting alone with Karen the Dog, wondering what am I going to do. You probably have a much better understanding at this point, as to some of the complexities in my recent life that have contributed to my difficulty in making this decision. You probably also are not sure as to *who* I am about to marry although I am certain that you could hazard a good guess. I could simply let the cat out of the bag right now but the woman I am to marry is allergic to cats and I truly do not wish to make her life any more difficult that I already have or than I am about to.

The cat may still be safely stowed away but the dog is out (sleeping soundly at my feet) so I'll throw you a bone…

You've already met her.

Something else an observant reader may have noticed and wondered about is why our nuptial guest list is as lopsided as the alignment of my $500,000 Stanc. Why does she have so many guests and I so few? And specifically why isn't Norm on the list? Good questions all but let me add another one that I still haven't answered – What exactly caused me to become an at least cautious believer in Forbes' picture of a random world?

"Why wasn't Norm invited to my wedding?" and "What exactly teetered me over the edge to become a believer of ROAR?" have the same answer so to expedite things, let's start with those.

*   *   *   *   *

In the beginning… I truly believed that I could make a difference. Some of my delusions even became reality. I was able to raise money for a reading center in the library of Seymour High School. We provided for the legal costs of a bookstore that was being asked by the police to reveal its sales records. We created a small business fund which helped start a day care center and an auto repair shop that provided jobs to homeless veterans.

The bookstore went bankrupt due to poor sales, the day care center closed amid accusations of child abuse and the auto repair shop closed after a local action reporter caught them on camera charging for repairs they didn't do. The day after the story broke about the auto repair shop, the action reporter himself was closed down when it was found out the he had fabricated facts in several stories he had previously worked on. The station fired him but aired the story about the auto repair shop because the video was just too darn good not to put on the air during sweeps weeks.

The reading center is still there, although I have to say I'm not sure anyone still uses it at all.

Most of these failures I didn't know about until recently. Back then, I had held these little victories hidden away, close to my heart like the one or two valued possessions of a homeless person. They brought me comfort as things began to unravel and now, I guess I'll just have to toss these little worthless gems in the pile of everything else that has unraveled at my feet.

Maybe, at this moment, someone is in the Reading Center at Seymour High reading this book. If you are, you have once again proven the cornerstone of the Forbes' "religion" and maybe, just ever-so-slightly shined one of the few remaining gems in my heart.

*   *   *   *   *

Someone once said, "Adventure is merely inconvenience rightly reconsidered." How to "rightly" consider what had happened to me was the trick and whether I looked at it from the right, left, top, bottom or from the back, my adventure was beginning to spill over with inconvenience.

And the spills seemed to become waves.

It seems, understandably so, that President Frank didn't care for the rumors about myself and his wife. Shortly after my visit to the White House, President Frank became ex-President Frank when he was stomped soundly in the next election. It seems that a crappy economy and unchecked corporate greed weighs more than nice hair and God Bless America verbiage on the scales of the American voters. God bless 'em. As an ex-president Frank did all the things you would expect of an ex-president – he established a library named after himself and went out on the lecture circuit, mostly in Europe and the Far East, charging an exorbitant amount of money for the privilege of passing him the sweet basil sauce and watching him drink from the finger bowl.

He also hired a man named Bo Bricker to make my life miserable. Bo was a dick. And I don't mean detective although he was that as well. Bo's job was basically to follow me around and to metaphorically stick burrs under my saddle, put pebbles in my shoes, put goo on my door handles and to light brown paper bags full of shit on my front porch.

He was a one man wave of inconvenience.

It wasn't long after Bo was brought on board the ex-president's payroll, when he found out about both Norm and Marcus. Despite my best efforts and wishes, my tidal wave of inconvenience splashed over onto them like a domesticated killer whale splashing children gathered round the walls of its see through tank.

I know this because I received regular letters, always typed and unsigned, that would inform me of events that were about to happen to my two friends but never in time for me to warn them. Norm received numerous parking tickets and moving violations and eventually had his license revoked. He drove anyway and eventually was arrested. On several occasions, Marcus was committed against his will into inpatient psychiatric care. This was not as bad as it sounds however since Marcus actually didn't mind spending time in the Crisis Unit, a fact that seemed to have slipped Bo Dick Bricker.

As for me, where ever I was, Bricker would leak to the press my location assuring a total lack of privacy. Clintonesque rumors regarding affairs and my sexual orientation found their way regularly into the more conservative media. My car was keyed. Once, and I swear this is true, I returned to my hotel room only to find that my bed had been short sheeted.

My first reaction was the classic "best defense is a good offense" line of thinking. I hired my own dick, and this time I do mean detective, a man by the name of Wink Gates, to hound

Bricker back to the butt hole that spawned him. In hindsight, what happen was predictable. I totally lost control of Wink as I would guess the ex-president lost control of Bricker. The two men escalated the war until it got out of hand and both Wink and Bricker ended up in the hospital. Wink was beaten until near death by an unknown assailant and one week later Bricker was cornered in an alley, attacked and sodomized by three steroid enhanced, oiled up body builders. I fired Wink over the phone as he lay in the hospital but I hear that to this day, he'll spit on the shoes of anyone who mentions Bricker's name.

Bricker, on the other hand, was a hard guy to dissuade. He was reeled in a little bit but he didn't go away. I guess it's easier for ex-presidents to find loyal help.

*   *   *   *   *

"While Little Tinkered in the White House, Friends Totter in the Nut House" read the headline of the National Enquirer. More of Bricker's work. The gist of the article was that I brought Marcus along to help me get into the White House and bonk the First Lady then dumped him and had him committed.

I was asked by a reporter from a more mainstream magazine how such articles fit in with the philosophy of ROAR. It was another one of those moments where I wished Forbes was still around because often as not, I was making shit up as I went.

148

By this time I'd had a decent understanding of the book and a better than average grasp of the underlying concepts.

Karen Eli Windslow had put me through ROAR boot camp consisting of 15 consecutive ten hour days of study and memorization overseen by Professor Amanda Took of the University of Southern Florida. Professor Took was a professor of philosophy who had her burst of fame when she was twelve as an Olympic gymnast. The clip of her fall off the balance beam which snapped her fibula in a compound fracture is still played during highlights of sports goriest moments.

I'm not great at memorization and I didn't do well. After the initial boot camp, I was ushered to weekly tutoring sessions and in time, I began to get a real feel for the material. I was issued quotes each week that I could reference when speaking , except I was to call them "passages" not "quotes". I was given briefings on how current events played into the ROAR philosophy. (When the Cubs won the series, even I could see a relationship.)

Occasionally however, a question would be asked that extended beyond my grasp of the material. These were seen as huge PR blunders by Karen (my agent, not Karen the Dog – she'd come around and always thought I was OK) and my tutoring session would be doubled the following week.

The problem with ROAR is that it didn't provide the "moral" map that other more traditional religions provided (and then often ignored). In addition to providing an explanation for things in general, most major religions came with a "users manual" if you will. Do this. Don't do that. ROAR had no such manual. Nowhere in its 210 pages did it ever say do not kill, do not confess to your dog's inter-species love affair on afternoon television. In fact the words "Do" and "Not" do not appear next to each other anywhere in the book.

"So, Mr. Little," the reporter asked again, "how do these personal attacks on you in the media fit in with the philosophy of ROAR?"

I was left with nothing. I couldn't say it was wrong – nothing in the book would back that up. I shrugged my shoulders and quoted perhaps the most famous anonymous philosopher of all times.

"Shit happens, I guess."

*   *   *   *   *

The more I didn't fight, the more I won.

The polls increasing showed people, particularly young adults in the 21 to 25 age bracket, were leaving traditional religions and stating ROAR as their belief of choice. Not only were the Catholics, Jews and other more traditional groups losing ground but so were the Hindus, Buddhists and other Eastern religions.

After the first 6 months or so of really stellar sales, we started the ROAR Hour, a Sunday morning cable show. We picked Sunday not because it had any significance within the ROAR philosophy but rather because we wanted a time slot where we could measure our progress. Almost all our competitors did their shows on Sunday, so that's when we did ours. The publicly published monthly TV ratings provided us with a free measuring stick of how we were stacking up against our various competitors.

And while all the other major religions were preaching "love thine enemy", they were pissed.

*   *   *   *   *

"We've got the contract with Lettem Inc. for the action figure and both the adult and children's versions of the board game." Karen was briefing me over the phone as she did every Monday and Thursday mornings. Although I couldn't see her, I had no doubt those driving near her vehicle on the highway, were in serious danger.

"Fuck off!"

"What?" I asked.

"Not you." She responded "Some asshole just flipped me off."

"That's a relief."

"What do you mean – 'That's a relief?'"

"For a second, I thought you saw me flipping you off through the phone somehow."

"You're a funny man Tom." She said, clearly not meaning it. "You have to know this stuff. Pay attention."

"We seriously have action figures?" I asked. "Of me?"

"Yes, of both you and Forbes. Forbes looks a little like Harrison Ford and I hope those personal training sessions we've scheduled have been paying off for you because you've got abs."

"Abs?"

"Yep, a six pack. It's the 21st century and the public will no longer buy an overweight Messiah so do more crunches."

"I'll add it to the list."

"There's more." She said.

"There is something better in life than having an action figure with six pack abs?"

"1.4 million times better, give or take a few hundred thousand." Her voice picked up. She was almost giddy. "We are just about to close a deal to have Thomas Little ROAR Toys in all Burger Barn Smiley Meals."

"You're kidding."

"Absolutely not. Collect all four. And you know what the best part is?" She didn't wait for an answer. "You never know which one you'll get. It's totally random."

*   *   *   *   *

The ironic part was that for the first time in my life, if the light was just right, I really had six pack abs. I had my own dietitian and personal trainer and had lost over 75 pounds. My teeth had been whitened, my skin tanned and my hair tastefully colored.

The irony within the irony though, was that I was beginning to like myself less than ever.

*   *   *   *   *

Radio debates were easy. In each city I'd visit, Karen would book me on some talk radio show with a toupeed host who's sole purpose in life was to pull the pins on grenades, throw them over the airwaves and stand back and watch them explode. Each of these guys (they were always guys) would come up with the original idea of putting me on the air with some local reverend to "debate" ROAR and what it stood for.

The most interesting thing about the debates, was that these religious minded men never attacked me on what I saw as the gaping hole in the "religion" that was ROAR.

It was not what it said. It was what it didn't say that was the problem with ROAR as a viable religion.

Unlike most religions, ROAR provided no moral compass for its flock. There was no list of rules that would occasionally be ignored but for the most part keep the flock in line and not killing each other or sleeping with their sisters and having deformed children. These preachers never nailed me on the lack of any "shalt nots" as Marcus later would. The radio preachers would invariably chose to make the debate into a argument on creationism and the origin of the species. My favorite was the argument that reflected my own original concerns and was typified by a preacher in Fargo who said, "There's no way that you can tell me that the wonderful creation that is our human existence was created by chance. The odds of that would have to be worse than one in a billion."

As I had come to learn, one in a billion happens all the time. Ask Bill Gates. What Forbes pointed out was that in an infinite universe, one in a billion, billion, billion happens all the time. There has been or will be a time when there will be someone exactly like Father Fargo, with the same greased back hair and bad teeth except he'll be wearing socks that match. It may not happen until after President Fisher actually admits he made a mistake but the universe will go on and on and on until it does happen. It has to. In an infinite universe every possibility is a certainty.

When who ever I was debating realized his socks didn't match or whatever else I could say that frustrated them, they would begin reciting scripture like it was... well, scripture. And I'd begin reciting from ROAR, which would burst the veins in their temples. I was beginning to realize however, that I really wasn't cut out to bust up their temples.

*   *   *   *   *

A beer mug sat full, flat and unpaid for.

Norm had been gone for 45 minutes which was long even by his standards and Marty the Bartender was a little concerned. There was a time when he would have simply dumped the beer, wiped the counter and hoped a customer who was going to tip him more than a quarter would sit down. But now, after irritating his way into the hearts of the staff, Norm always had a place to sit. Since it had come out that he'd been with me on my first foray into the White House and his resulting radio bit, he had become somewhat of a local, minor celebrity. For Marty the Bartender this was particularly nice, since Norm rarely had to pay for his beer and whoever picked up the tab for him would tip better than Norm. Things had a way of working out in a random universe.

Today however, there wasn't anyone in the bar so Norm's absence was conspicuous. Marty asked a manger to watch the bar for a minute and went off to see where Norm had wandered to and to lead him back to the bar or to his car, whichever Norm fussed less about.

The search didn't take long because as Marty headed for the door, Norm came walking in holding a hand to his chest, looked directly at Marty and said, "What's your name again?"

"Norm, my name is Marty. I've worked here for three years."

"Well Marty, who's worked here for three years, somebody shot me and I need a beer."

Norm walked to the bar, pulled himself up on his stool reached out and drank the entire mug, leaving red fingerprints of blood on the glass.

*   *   *   *   *

Norm had no idea who had shot him or why. He said the man looked at him a moment and then just shot him for no reason. My initial guess was that it was a mugger and the guy

156

looked him over once and realized mugging Norm would be a waste of his time.

Despite the attacker's best efforts, Norm not only lived but his injuries were minor. In the chest pocket of his shirt, Norm had been carrying the Bible he had stolen from the hotel room we had stayed in on our way to D.C. months before. It seems the bullet hit the Bible which slowed it down to the point that it barely broke the skin. So other than a flesh wound and few slightly bruised ribs, Norm walked away none the worse for wear.

His celebrity status at the Hideaway had hit an all time high.

*   *   *   *   *

A sign from God that the Bible was His true Word and was the vehicle of salvation for us all or... another example of the inevitable certainty of even the strangest possibility in a random world?

Either way, it resulted in two important events. First, Norm has refused to attend my wedding in part, because he is afraid. The primary reason he's not coming is because he's forgotten about it. The second result of Norm's close call is that Norm has never left his room without a Bible in his shirt pocket and says he won't for the rest of his life. I asked him once if he found comfort in the words there. He told me he found more comfort in its ability to stop bullets.

*　　*　　*　　*　　*

Marty the Bartender's last name was Turner. He had a younger sister, Sky Turner who became the lover of Kelly Windslow, Karen Eli Windslow's suicidal younger sister whom we talked about earlier. Today, they live together on a ranch in Wyoming and never responded to the RSVP with my wedding invitation. Maybe they know something I don't.

*　　*　　*　　*　　*

Karen came to my door and knocked the knock of someone who doesn't believe they should be knocking, quick raps that let the person inside know that they should have been waiting with the door open. Karen the Dog barked a reply that was equally impatient while I was in the bathroom, worrying about hair growing from my ears.

Karen the Dog never did warm up to Karen the Agent (Now that I think about it, Karen the "Person" seems to be stretching it a bit) so I let her (the dog) out back and opened up the front door.

"So glad to see you Tom." Karen said and hugged me. "This is Brad Stiensky. Brad this is Thomas Little." The man moved his cigarette from his hand to the corner of his mouth and extended his hand.

I took it and shook it, inviting them in at the same time. Brad Stiensky looked like my college roommate freshman year, curly black hair with an attempt at an "artsy unconcerned" look by sporting an unsuccessful attempt at facial hair. He was easily half as old as I was.

"Karen, you do not bring me guests unless they are talented or useful. So which is he?"

"In this case, it's both." She responded. "Brad is a director."

"Really?" It slipped out before I could contain it. Brad looked like he just finished filming a cut with his camcorder for "America's Backyard Wrestling Stunts and Crashes"

"Yes," Brad jumped in not looking at me. "I've directed a number of videos and am looking to do something more… more substantial."

"Any films?" I asked

"Ha." His head rolled back and for a second seemed to threaten to fall off his neck. He shook his head and looked around for an astray to snuff out his cigarette. "Films are so fucking commercial. Product placements, dealing with dumb fuck studio execs. Not for me. No, Not for me. Plus, this project intrigues me. Randomness lends itself to visuals. Like the book says… 'Circles of order in a roaring endless stream of randomly rushing water.' That's beautiful."

I didn't have any ashtrays and didn't offer to solve his problem for him. He stuck the butt back in his mouth.

"I've hired Brad to assist you in creating a documentary film on ROAR." Karen said. "Something edgy that would help explain it to the kids."

"Since when have kids become fans of documentaries?" I asked.

"They haven't," She said, "but they will when they see this one. It'll play in megaplexes, not on the nature channel."

I didn't even bother to think out the logic because if Karen had gone this far with the idea, I knew that she must have already researched it, tested it and was absolutely sure it would fly. If Karen said a project would work, you could be sure it would work… and that it would make her enough money to warrant her efforts.

"Did you say help *me*?"

"Yes, you will be directing the piece." She said.

I noticed Brad was looking at the ground.

"I don't know squat about directing…"

"And that is why Brad is here. Our marketing profile of you as a renaissance man needs a boost. You can direct."

Both Brad and I knew it had been decided and would be the way Karen wanted it.

"While I have you here, I thought you might want to know." I said. "Norm was shot yesterday."

She paused for a micro-second.

"I guess tt looks like we've made it." She said smiling. She gathered up her purse and her director and left.

*   *   *   *   *

I stood in the doorway as Karen and Brad drove off. As they rounded the corner, a convertible Saab came from the opposite direction, pulled into my driveway and parked next to my Stanc. Colleen Fisher stepped out. I waited for her with the door open.

After predictable pleasantries, Colleen told me why she had come. She had received a threat. It seems the Scientific Church of Light was unhappy with the market share that ROAR was taking from them. When I checked the numbers later with Karen, I'd find out that one third of the S.C.L. flock had flown south for ROAR. As Karen later put it, this "represented a significant loss of income" and they had no choice but to respond.

It showed how far ROAR had come. They were all responding - the Catholics, the Baptists, the Jews. Even the pacifistic, far-easterner organizations were issuing statements implying that ROAR was not a worthy adversary. You don't issue statements about adversaries that are not worthy.

The greatest resentment seemed to flow from the fact that Karen didn't play by the rules of traditional religion. She embraced opinion polls, took out billboards, advertised, created profit generating cost centers, actively sought to grab market share (had she had me say "convert nonbelievers" perhaps things would have been different.) Not since the Catholics of centuries long past had anyone so aggressively sought to establish a religious organization.

And it was beginning to tick people off.

"I got a phone call, several actually." Colleen said. "The first two were a man's voice. Mostly questions, 'How well do you know Thomas Little? Are you a member of ROAR?' Both calls ended with 'If you know what's good for you, you will talk to Mr. Little and help him see the error of his ways"

"They really said 'If you know what's good for you'?"

"Yeah, it gets better. Do you know how I know it's the Scientific Church of Light?"

"You're kidding..." I said.

"Yep, Caller ID."

While they didn't come right out and threaten Colleen's life, the Scientific Church of Light made it overwhelmingly clear that something bad would happen if ROAR did not change its ways and play by the rules. SCL had been the newest kid on the block so it made sense that they would be the ones most threatened. They had the most to lose.

We were standing in the kitchen and I shared with Colleen what had happened to Norm.

"Now it makes me wonder if Norm's little incident might not have been a mugging after all." I said as I reached for two glasses. "Would you like a drink?"

"Yes, please." Colleen said "But no one shot at me."

"But they threatened you?"

"Did Norm get a threat before they shot him?" She asked.

Did I mention that Colleen Fisher was in the midst of a very public divorce from the former President? Did I mention that she was wearing a very professional looking skirt with a top that clung to her body like the dust on my martini glasses? Did I mention that she had let her hair grow out, had absolutely perfect teeth and was wearing just the right amount of lipstick? I may not have. Those thoughts and others like them, kept slipping around behind my eyes, through my ears and down to where I could taste them on the tip of my tongue.

"No, I don't think Norm received any threats." I said finally. "Although I'm not sure he would remember if he had."

My inner thoughts must have slipped out of my head and onto my face because she looked down into her drink with a kind of a smile.

"Did you ever get caught sneaking out of the White House?" I asked.

"Not really." She said. "I'm fairly sure Frank knew about it but he never said anything."

"Being the prophet of the hour is beginning to taste a little like milk in a warm glass. I have a renewed appreciation for your former dilemma."

"My current dilemma isn't much better. Frank is being an ass about this whole divorce. To the point where he's scaring me a little. And the press is still around every corner looking for some kind of dirt that they can spin into a story. At least within the walls of the White House I had some sort of refuge. Now… it seems like everywhere is fair game for them."

"Aren't we the pair." I said. At which point I leaned across and kissed her for the first time.

* * * * *

Was that the whisker of the proverbial cat poking out of proverbial bag?

*   *   *   *   *

Keeping secrets has never been a strong suit for me.

Let's fast forward a bit. Colleen kissed me back. Eventually, we hooked up, fell in love, I proposed and we have a wedding planned for tomorrow. She is the most unlikely, wonderful, intelligent and beautiful woman I have ever known. Remember the church with curvature of the spine? I still haven't found a cure.

There. That feels better. Now I'll say my three Hail Marys and we're done.

Except I'm still thinking that I'm not going.

*   *   *   *   *

Avoidance - another major human motivator. We often do a lot to not do something little. Up to now I've avoided mentioning the 'The Portal". In my defense, I have stuck in a few articles so you wouldn't be totally behind. Time to face the music and catch up with the plot of this opera.

In a nut shell, this "hole", for lack of a better description, simply showed up in Orlando. Nobody is exactly sure of the exact date. To the best of my knowledge, it had nothing to do with me, with ROAR or Forbes, with the Hideaway, with Norm or Marcus or, despite what follows, even with Karen Eli Windslow.

However, "it" showed up shortly after ROAR showed up in the same city and roughly the same time. Talk about your major "swirling pool of chance" in a random world. Assuming that this phenomenon could have appeared in any four square feet of Earth, the odds of it appearing within the Orlando city limits at the exact moment in time Karen and I were championing the Religion of Absolute Randomness are... well, astounding. (Forbes was the math whiz but since he'd passed away I've had people on staff who calculated stuff like that for me.)

But let's back up a step. What exactly is the "Rabbit Hole of Robinson Street"? It is a two dimensional, perfectly round hole in space which emits no light or sound. It has no thickness, odor, weight or political allegiance. At first glance, it appears to be a vertical hole in the alley side wall of the brick office of the Hoover Brothers Destruction Company. However, in reality, it is actually hovering in space 6.25 inches away from the brick. This

6.25 inches would later become very important in a lawsuit brought forth by the Hoover Brothers claiming ownership of the hole.

Why would a destruction company want to claim ownership to a flat, four foot diameter wrinkle in space? Because of the most unique and fascinating property of the hole – nothing that went into the hole ever came out.

Ever.

You could pass your hand across the black plain and your arm would disappear from sight, seemingly cut off at the angle on which you inserted it. The good news was that you could withdraw your arm and it would be totally unharmed. However, if you made the same mistake as Dante Garcia and Jose Murphy, Darby Hayes and several of the authorities who arrived early on the scene, and jumped completely across the surface of the "hole", you would never be heard from again.

Ever.

Or at least not yet anyway.

Any stone, penny, mobster, watch, condom or radio active waste inserted into the hole would also disappear with an equal permanency.

The fact that this "Portal of Permanent Elimination" ended up behind a destruction company... well, the Hoover Brothers certainly felt it meant something. 6.25 inches, however, while not enough to get you porn work, was enough for the court to rule that the hole was technically above the alley which was public property and that the Hoover brothers had no right to it.

*   *   *   *   *

Just to make sure I haven't missed anything, up to this point, what we have is this:

- An unemployed assessment specialist, a retired, semi-senile old man and a black man with a sense of humor and schizophrenia sneak into the White House through tunnels long forgotten and end up meeting the President and more importantly, the First Lady of the United States of America.

- A somewhat backward psychologist/author pens a book entitled "ROAR - The Religion of Absolute Randomness" and then electrocutes himself trying to massage his back in the bathtub with the Shitsu Electric Super Massager.

- The unemployed assessment specialist, under the guidance of a medusa headed, money worshiping agent, picks up the flag, and turns the book into a "Book" and creates a religion with a marketing plan.

- The same unemployed assessment specialist, now gainfully employed as a Savior, falls in love with the First Lady who has divorced the President. (Who is now a jealous ex-President with lots of time on his hands.)

- Other, more traditional Religion organizations see ROAR as a direct threat to their market share and begin to form committees to develop business plans to address the threat by thinking "out of the box".

- The retired semi-senile old man is shot but survives due to the bullet being stopped by the stolen Bible he had stuck in his pocket.

- And in the meantime, the ultimate tourist attraction, a mysterious and unexplainable "hole in space" shows up in the backyard of Mickey and Shamu, causing ride planners in several major theme parks to be fired for not having come up with the idea first.

Yeah, I think that's about it.

*   *   *   *   *

Shortly after the Black Hole was discovered it was roped off and guarded around the clock. Not knowing exactly what it was, scientists were taking no chances. They wanted no one near the thing. It was probed but any instrument completely placed into the hole disappeared like anything else and any tool dangled in the hole, while remaining attached to something on the real world side of the things, simply stopped measuring whatever it was designed to measure the moment it passed inside.

As you can imagine, the news of the hole's existence had a variety of effects throughout the world. One of the more unfortunate of these effects was the draw it had on certain individuals who felt a need to pass through the hole themselves. The last of the 12 known individuals who actually made it past the early security and into the hole, was Darby Hayes.

According to friends quoted in the paper, Darby was depressed and recently unemployed. Like everything else that totally crossed the plain of the opening, Darby completely disappeared and was never seen again.

Ever.

Darby had just been fired from his job as a ride designer for a local theme park.

Some swirling pools of chance are a little easier to swallow than others.

*   *   *   *   *

"The Portal."

That is what the mysterious black hole of Robinson Street eventually became known as. It is interesting because it implies passage of some sort – an opening going from one place to another. The reality is that we really only knew the first place, an alley in Florida. There is not only zero evidence regarding what the second place may have looked like, there is no evidence that a second place even existed at all. It is equally as plausible that The Portal wasn't an opening at all but rather a big garbage disposal that simply transformed matter as we know it into something we don't understand as of yet. Or maybe a mass delusion? A dream in the mind of a man who has succumbed to stress and exhaustion and fallen asleep on the eve of his wedding?

*   *   *   *   *

Flowers were another side effect of The Portal. At first, it seemed that they were in memory of the missing boys but they never stopped. Outside the barricades they started piling up into botanical mountain ranges. Roses, daisies, daffodils, wildflowers, flowers of every imaginable type were laid gently outside The Portal.

I was never sure if the flowers were looking backward in remembrance or forward in hope. My guess is that the people who put them there didn't really know either. Either way, we took care of them. I had my staff give out free iced tea and water to all visitors and we made sure that the flowers remained undisturbed. Karen made sure that we had a ROAR banner across our drink stand.

*   *   *   *   *

"My" documentary film outlining the Religion of Absolute Randomness was truly a work of cinematography. The fact that I had very little to do with its creation didn't mean I couldn't appreciate it as art. I was on the set when it was filmed. I even said "Action!" and "Cut!" more than once (With the obligatory "Behind the Scenes" photographers recording the moment for the cable special.) but all the creative decisions were Brad's. This will be big news if and when anyone actually reads this. It will also likely result in me losing my Academy Award. It's only fair. I did admit that I stole the award as part of my acceptance speech but I never should have accepted it in the first place. I'd give the statue back but as I mentioned earlier, it's been spray painted and I haven't seen it since the last time Marcus visited.

I *can* take credit for two ideas that actually made it into the film. Neither contributed much to the quality of the project or to its artistry. One of the two ideas however, ended up having a rather profound affect in another way, although I hadn't intended it.

My first suggestion was to film The Portal and use the footage as part of the opening and closing sequences. I was playing art student and just generally getting in the way of the people who were really making the film when I blurted out that the famous "doorway" could symbolize an entrance into the film. It was one of those moments when people just kind of look at each other, shrug their shoulders and smile at that fact that the most clueless member of the group actually came up with a plausible idea.

It wasn't until after the film came out that the real impact of my suggestion became apparent. Because of it's place in the film and because of its timely appearance just as ROAR was blossoming as a religion, The Portal somehow became synonymous in many people's minds with ROAR. It became a icon that Karen Eli Windslow took up like a cash deposit dropped from the back of a Brinks truck and ran with like hell. From its second printing forward, an iconic version of The Portal was on the cover of Forbes' famous book. It was a part of every commercial and in the opening sequence of all of our infomercials. They even started including a mini version of it made out of a round piece of black vinyl with my action figure.

And its all a coinquidink. I wish I could say that I had the foresight to have seen the impact of The Portal on our little endeavor but I didn't.

My second contribution to the film was less earth shattering but important to me none the less. I got Norm a bit part in the background of the second longest scene in the film. He was sitting quietly. At a bar. Staring at his beer. The happiest I'd ever seen Norm was when we finally premiered the film, seeing himself on screen for the first time. I'm sure he felt that he'd be the talk of the all the ladies at the home. I hope he was.

*   *   *   *   *

So you may be wondering, where was Marcus during my clanking rollercoaster ride up the hills of fame? Marcus, my friend of dubious brain chemistry, of a decidedly non presidential sense of humor and my only potential wedding guest?

I'm glad you asked.

174

*   *   *   *   *

But first, another Marcus story. I believe I already told you that Marcus was a veteran and expert marksman. Way back when, when I was still in the assessing business, the only information I was able to find out about Marcus' military record was self reported. He told me he had been honorably discharged after only one year of service. Now not having ever served in the military, this seemed strange to me because I thought the minimum length of service was at least two years. Stating you had only served a year isn't something that even the most delusional of people would come up with. Its just too boring of a fact to be a delusion. Based on my intial assessment of him however, it appeared that Marcus clearly believed it to be true.

Later, after I moved from Marcus' assessor to his roommate, I was helping him gather together some documentation to help him grease the wheels of the covered wagon of a bureaucracy that was the mental health system. Things like picture IDs, a copy of a birth certificate and an official copy of military records can move things along if you happen to decompensate and start believing you're Sadam Hussain. During that process I found out that he had indeed been honorably discharged after one year. He had also received a written commendation for his work as a sentry where it was noted he had an especially keen eye for spotting camouflaged enemy snipers. On a second sheet of paper dated a month or so later it was noted that he continued to spot enemy snipers camouflaged in trees outside the field hospital. He continued to spot them in the military psychiatric hospital upon his return to California.

After never firing a shot or being fired upon and receiving written commendation for his delusions, Marcus was quietly discharged with full benefits.

*   *   *   *   *

So, what was happening with my friend as my name was becoming a household word?

After Marcus moved out of my place, he headed south to Key West and became an urban camper for a while.

I've worked with social workers who step out of their SUVs each morning holding their five dollar mocha cappuccinos while talking on their cell phones on the way to their offices. If you stop them and ask them about homelessness, they will tell you that no one, ever, chooses to be homeless. If someone says otherwise they are either rationalizing homelessness in our society or are too naive or mentally ill to know otherwise. The concept of someone not wanting or needing a Chrysler, Starbucks or Motorola was impossible for them to understand.

Marcus often went urban camping. It was easier than wilderness camping because you didn't need a tent and food was always near by. The wildlife was perhaps slightly more dangerous (Suburban teenagers kill more people than bears do.) but when you sleep in a park with your eyes closed it looks the same as sleeping beneath a tree on the side of a mountain. My guess, and it's admittedly only a semi-educated guess because Marcus and I never really talked about it, is that many of us have a need to be unencumbered and feel totally in charge of ourselves. If you're rich enough, you hire a guide and climb Mount Kilimanjaro. If you're less well to do, you buy a motorcycle. But if you have little money and enough balls to take the risk, there is something about not being tied to anyone or anything that takes you to a similar place.

Now I may be exaggerating the experience somewhat but Marcus could always spend the night at my place and he often chose not to. My sense was that if Marcus had been born 100 years earlier, he would have been a fur trapper – men who were also technically homeless. There have always been men and women who choose to live on the fringe of every society. Today however, there is no longer a geographic fringe, only a social one and if you wanted to live on the fringe as an urban camper there was perhaps no place better to do it than in the Florida Keys.

Sun, tourists and services. Melanoma, spare change and anti-psychotics. What more could you want?

Marcus, while cursed with a mental disorder that cost him a certain amount of control over his brain chemistry, was equally blessed with an abnormal amount of control over his body. He could reduce his heartbeat by concentrating on his breathing. He had an unusually high pain threshold. However, his most interesting and definitely most profitable, physical talent was his extraordinary degree of flexibility. He could contort his limbs into a pretzel. He could twist himself in ways that made him look like the wires behind an old computer.

Now these talents came in handy for Marcus in a number of ways. While he rarely spent time in psychiatric hospitals and even more rarely required restraint while he was there, on the few occasions when they did try to restrain him, it rarely worked. They would strap him down in five-point restraints and return 15 minutes later only to find Marcus sitting on the bed biting his toe nails. Had Marcus been born a few years earlier and somehow met up with an agent further down on Karen Eli Windslow's family money tree, he would have been the perfect guest on the Ed Sullivan show. Unfortunately for Marcus, the market for professional contortionists has pretty much dried up almost everywhere in the world that has indoor plumbing. Everywhere that is, except Key West.

In Key West, on Mallory Square, as the apple sun dips itself into the caramel waters of the Gulf of Mexico, the tourists in Jimmy Buffett parrot head hats and bright flowered shirts, slide off the sweaty seats of electric buses, take out their wallets and show their appreciation for the finer arts – like cat trainers, fire eaters, three card montyists, ladder walking chainsaw jugglers and contortionists.

Marcus had a job for 15 minutes, on Thursday, Friday, and Saturday nights. He made enough in 45 minutes a week with his ankles behind his neck, to live the mocha-less lifestyle he sought.

*   *   *   *   *

If we could somehow be shrunk ala the Fantastic Voyage and be allowed to enter the brain baggage of the over rich, over weight, over bearing tourists who made up most of Marcus' audience, I wonder what percent we would find that had a synapse snap along the lines of … "I wonder if that guy can give himself a blow job?" Ninety percent? Ninety five percent? For the record, I never asked. It wasn't part of the assessment.

*   *   *   *   *

Although he never figured out a way to profit from it, another interesting fact about my friend Marcus was that he had six toes on each foot. Just like Hemingway's cats, the descendents of which still roam Key West. Yet another spinning pool of coincidence.

*   *   *   *   *

When I first met Marcus back at Seaside, they put him in restraints in our psych unit. He got out and was biting his toenails. I assumed they didn't bother putting him back because they thought he'd just escape again. Rich Hayes, a Psych Tech on duty that night told me later that the head nurse on duty told them to "string him up again." Except when they opened the door, the sight of someone chewing on his sixth toe grossed Rich and his partner out so much that they decided to ignore the Charge Nurse and to just leave Marcus alone. Rich later took a job as an attendant at Golden Age Retirement Home but was fired when he was accused of abuse by outraged investigative reporter Lawrence Ledbetter. The station apparently didn't think it could get the ratings it wanted with the follow-up story. If they had done the story, it would have shown that after an extensive investigation Rich was found innocent of the charge. They didn't seem interested. They also weren't interested in his difficulties in finding work after the erroneous piece

… or his subsequent break up from his girlfriend.

… or his suicide.

*   *   *   *   *

Marcus's life in Key West was simple but going better than even he had imagined it would. The weather was perfect. He eventually even found a friend who was letting him sleep in his basement. He had a bed. He didn't have a TV. His sunset performances were being well received by both the tourists and perhaps more importantly by the close knit community of street people and performance artists that called Key West their home.

And then…

"Bang"

Everything changed

Again.

*   *   *   *   *

It was a Sunday night. Marcus usually didn't do Sunday nights but he had had a slow weekend and had heard that several of the regular performers wouldn't be at the Square. His performance was going well and he had a decent crowd. Or so he thought at first. As he finished extracting himself from the two foot by two foot box that served as the only prop in his act, he noticed two men in particular in the audience. He knew beyond a shadow of a doubt that these two men were FBI. I later asked him how he could be so sure, was it the clothes? The way they acted?

Marcus said he just knew… "From years of experience."

He also knew that he would have to do something.

The finale for Marcus' act has always been something he called "The Human Goodyear." Marcus would lift his ankles behind his neck and then extend and flex his limbs to form a wheel out of himself. He would then ask a member of the audience to lift him up and roll him around much to the delight and amusement of the crowd. Once he got moving, he'd ask his volunteer to stop and he'd roll on his own for a short while and then wobble down, much the way a hub cap would come to rest after being thrown from an old Stanc. He'd finally come to rest circling his tip can which he would then immediately pick up and start distributing to the crowd.

That was how it usually went. On this particular Sunday night, with two not so enthusiastic FBI agents in the crowd, Marcus had other ideas. As the two men moved closer to the stage, Marcus sensed his act was about to be abruptly ended. He called up a large man with a flowing white beard and leather chaps as his volunteer to help him with his big finish. Marcus rolled himself up and had the volunteer give him an unusually good push. However, instead of leaning to one side, which would normally result in him rolling in circles, Marcus stayed straight up and down as possible. This caused him to roll straight down the pier.

As he rolled, he picked up speed and much to the amazement of his audience, his fellow performers and the two FBI agents, Marcus continued to roll until he launched off the end of the pier and splashed into the spinning eddies of the ocean below.

*   *   *   *   *

According to everyone who was present that day, the Human Goodyear disappeared and he has never again been seen performing before the setting Caribbean sun.

*   *   *   *   *

Marcus rolled and rolled like a vinyl heavy metal record, listening to the music that only he could hear, away from the FBI and off the edge of the concrete pier. What he hadn't considered was the fact that the depth of the water just off the pier was only two and a half feet deep. After a fall of approximately twenty feet, while your body is twisted into the shape of a wheel, two and half feet not only wasn't much, it wasn't enough. Marcus crashed in to the water and a split second later crashed into the concrete just below the water, knocking himself unconscious. The tide pulled him out, away from the pier and the waves took him in like a huge washing machine. They churned him and spun him though the heavy wash cycle and spit him out like heavy cotton.

The next memory he had was of looking up at a naked penis.

It seems he'd been washed down shore and had come to rest on the beach at a local nudist resort where a man was standing over him. The penis and the man, while obviously concerned about Marcus' well being, were not particularly what Marcus expected to see.

"Get the fuck away from me." Or something to that effect was Marcus' response to the actions of the good, but very naked, Samaritan.

"Are you OK?" the man persisted. This was apparently one truly kind soul of a naked man.

"I'm friggin fine with the exception of your dick hanging in my face, the fact that the FBI is going to arrest my ass, and that I have a headache the size of the Gulf of Mexico.

"There's no FBI here." Said the naked man, "You're safe here."

"Really? Then why don't you do me favor and take yourself and your little pecker and leave me the fuck alone."

"Now, come on. Chill out. Its OK."

"Hell no, its not OK!" Marcus said. "There are people after me and I have some homo dancing over me with his prick dangling in my face. I'm what you would call very far from being OK."

Now it doesn't take a licensed psychotherapist to see that Marcus' behavior would be seen as a little eccentric even by what were likely liberal, nude vacationers in Key West, Florida. It wasn't long before the police were called and shortly after that Marcus was transported to the local inpatient psych unit. Upon admission he was assessed by an Assessment Specialist, very much like I was once upon a day. When asked, "So, Marcus, what's going on here?" His first response would be…

"Fuck you! There is no fucking way I'm going to listen to you. I'm being followed by the FBI and unless you release me immediately, I will be arrested and likely killed."

Needless to say, he was promptly committed to 72 hours of observation in the hospital where he was heavily medicated and, no doubt, frustrated his captors by eluding any attempts to restrain him .

*　　　*　　　*　　　*　　　*

Of course, the irony is that Marcus really was being followed by the FBI this time. Although it was highly unlikely that he would have been killed and certainly no one was actually stealing his socks and using them to obtain his DNA, which was one of the statements dutifully documented on the Intake Assessment Form 123-IAF-4-04.

*   *   *   *   *

If I were to take you right now, onto the roof of a 20 story building and walk you to the edge, you would be standing there looking down over 200 ft at the pavement below. If I were then to tell you that, if you were to jump, you would be fine. If I were to promise you that it was so, that the laws of nature had been temporarily suspended and that if you jumped you would glide gracefully down to the ground, totally unharmed. You would look at me and say...

"Fuck you! There is no fucking way I'm listening to you." Or something culturally appropriate to the same affect.

The point being that when someone with schizophrenia hears voices, they don't' simply "think" they hear voices, they actually hear voices. When they say they see eyeballs on the walls, they really do see eyeballs on the walls. So when Marcus feels like he's in danger, he'll say "Fuck you" in a very similar manner to the way you would say it to me on our hypothetical roof.

*   *   *   *   *

Ex-President Frank Fisher was not adjusting well to life after the White House. I would guess that after being Commander-in-Chief of the most powerful nation in the world, it would be hard for anyone to settle down and content themselves with ordering the help around. However for Frank Fisher, a man who had never taken an order from anyone other than his father, a man who started setting goals with detailed measurable objectives in the second grade, a man who would be class president Fisher, quarterback Fisher, point guard Fisher, CEO Fisher, Chairmen Fisher, Governor Fisher and President Fisher, it was a particularly difficult transition.

To be set aside on the mantel like a treasured keepsake but left out of the action was possibly the worst imaginable fate for a man like Frank. He hadn't realized that even he would become less useful to the powers that be. As Colleen later quoted him… Hell, he WAS the powers that be. However, the conservative power base had to move on to new battles and Frank clearly was not the general behind whom they would rally. They needed him to stand in the background and smile, perhaps say some of the things the new generals wanted to say but could not afford to say publicly. They needed him to wave at parades and give stirring but meaningless speeches at rallies. They needed him to parrot the new party line and help the party win the geriatric vote.

He felt impotent.

The fact that he was, didn't help.

*　　　*　　　*　　　*　　　*

No, Frank Fisher would not go quietly into the night. He would not become the kindly grandfather of the Republican Party. First, he was too young and felt he still had "gas in the tank". Second, his wife had left him and he had lost the election. These were the only two failures he had ever experienced and he needed a pound of flesh. He needed several pounds.

190 pounds.

Shaped just like me.

I was in great shape by this point in my story.

With the help of modern science, I had even begun to grow back some hair.

*　　　*　　　*　　　*　　　*

Now, I know enough to not flatter myself by implying that Ex-President Frank Fisher had set his sights on me because of my accomplishments or my deeds. No, it would be apparent to any pimpled, first year psych student that Frank's rage went much deeper. I was however, by this time a very public target that seemed to symbolize to Frank everything that he despised. I hadn't earned my place in the world and the basic tenets of "The Religion of Absolute Randomness" seemed to stick out its tongue at the unquestionable traditional Anglo-American, conservative Christian values that Frank clung to as the foundation of his being.

Equally important, after him leaving office and his wife leaving him, Frank was in charge of nothing. I pictured him sitting around the house in his pajamas, sipping coffee, reading the paper, looking out the window, sitting down again, looking in the refrigerator for the fifth time, drinking right out of the milk carton (a crime which of course he would deny) and then looking out the window again. The man had to be bored out of his mind. His life was a vacuum equaled in size only by his ego.

So my role as the can on the fence at the end of Frank's personal shooting gallery was partially due perhaps to poor parenting, partially due to boredom and probably more than partially due to the fact that I was spending more and more time with his ex-wife.

*   *   *   *   *

Colleen and I had been dating for about six months before I finally asked her the big question.

"So, I was wondering," I began hesitantly "Do you believe in ROAR?"

She was folding laundry, a simple chore that she seemed to enjoy.

"There really isn't much there to believe in, is there?" She said continuing to fold.

"Millions of people seem to think so."

"I guess they do. But many, many people once believed in Zeus and Aphrodite too. It didn't make them right."

My mind wondered for a moment at the fact that out of all the gods and goddesses she could have chosen she chose the one most closely associated with sex. I was liking this woman more all the time.

"So, do you believe in God?" I asked.

"Who is asking, the press? A highly placed official of the Religion of Absolute Randomness? My mother?

"Does it matter?"

"No, not really. Same answer, just different packages."

"Just me." I said.

190

She was now folding her underwear. There is something important about the stage of a relationship when a woman is comfortable enough with you to allow you to see her fold her underwear. I don't think that she will be too upset with me if I tell you that they were not the kind of underwear you'd expect a former First Lady to be wearing.

"Is there a God?" She repeated the question. "Perhaps, but there doesn't have to be."

Her answer explained a lot to me. I still didn't know why she was with me but at least I knew how it was that she could live with my job. While she wasn't part of the kneeling masses who were throwing themselves at the Religion of Absolute Randomness, she did feel it made sense. As she would later tell me, she believed in half of the acronym – she didn't see ROAR as a "religion" and the word "absolute" in regards to anything made her uncomfortable. She was however, very comfortable with "randomness."

She also apparently had no problem with the word "of".

*   *   *   *   *

Six months ago the Hoover Brothers Destruction Company was hired by the federal government to destroy the main offices of the Hoover Brothers Destruction Company.

The actual implosion was carried out with an unusual amount of care and precision, certainly a great deal more than when they destroyed Seaview back when I worked there. When they blew Seaview sky high, not only were they not worried if a stray brick or piece of plaster flew through the air, the movie producers filming the event insisted on it. In comparison, when the Hoover Brothers imploded their own office, it was monitored by over one hundred members of various arms of the Federal Government. Furthermore, even though it will never grace the screens of your local megaplex, there were no fewer than eighteen cameras filming the event.

The reason for all the attention was, of course, because the now famous "Portal" was located only six inches from the back of the Hoover Brother's office. The fact that any debris, which may have accidentally been blown into the "hole", would have instantly disappeared seemed lost on the scientists that surrounded, observed, monitored and measured the event in every way possible. The government scientists in charge of the project didn't know what would happen should the explosion spill over into The Portal and dealt with their sense of powerlessness by watching, as if watching the event more closely somehow made it safer.

True to their reputation, the Hoover Brothers destroyed their own headquarters with the same precision that they had displayed in destroying 343 other structures - with exception of course, of the aforementioned Seaview explosion. This one went down without a hitch and it was just the first. Eventually, every other building within 300 feet of the Portal was also cremated with equal efficiency.

The entire area was now under the control of the Department of Homeland Security and was now sealed off tighter than Tupperware.

$$* \qquad * \qquad * \qquad * \qquad *$$

While Karen Eli Windslow turned The Portal into an icon for the Religion of Absolute Randomness, the scientific community was trailing behind, doing its best to explain the phenomenon. The obvious problem was that in order to explain something, you had to understand it. In order to understand it, you had to have something to analyze.

The difficulty the scientific community was having in explaining The Portal wasn't so much in the inability to gather data, there was some data to be had, but more in the scarcity of the data. It didn't help that a fourth grader with a tape measure could gather all the data regarding The Portal as well and as quickly as an MIT graduate.

The facts:

- It was about 4 feet in diameter. (3.94329 feet to be exact and to give at least a little nod to the MIT crowd.)

- It was about 6 inches off the ground. (Again, not exactly. It was 6.000145 inches off the ground as measured by Danny Lowe, the post graduate student initially assigned to the project.)

- It's "thickness" was unable to be measured. When viewed from the side, it disappeared.

- It was black in color from both sides. (Black as in a total absence of color.)

- If matter completely crossed the plane without being connect to matter on "our" side of the plane – it disappeared. Forever.

- Once matter disappeared it never reappeared.

And that's it.

No temperatures, no other distances, no times, no odors, no sounds, no radiation, no emissions either visible or otherwise.

When your job is developing theories and formulating hypotheses and when a whole nation is waiting on your every word, this is not a lot to go on. Several well known physicists, astronomers, mathematicians and even a biologist or two took their shots at attempting to tie the phenomenon in with other current theories with minimal success. They all, at some point in their arguments, had to resort to guessing and bending the existing thinking beyond the breaking point. Like piranha, their supposed peers devoured them like a fawn making an innocent attempt to ford a stream.

The Portal simply could not be explained by any currently understood scientific explanation.

Scientists however, are generally a patient bunch. They don't totally get gravity or why sub atomic particles behave the way they do but, for the most part, scientists are willing to wait and watch. They are confident that the evidence will eventually turn up just has it has over and over through out history. Our world of immediate gratification however, is not so patient.

What was hard to accept was that The Portal was such a departure from everything we had egotistically thought we knew. Prior to its appearance, the pieces of the scientific Lego set of the universe were just starting to look like they were falling together. Now, groups of egg headed theorists were sitting confused among their beakers and chalkboards and were beginning to think that they may have to scrap a century's worth of head scratching and start over. For some of the older men and women in lab coats, it was too much to bear. Universities and government labs all over the world saw a significant spike in early retirements. (At least the scientists who measured retirement rates still had something to measure.) School budgets took a hit as text books were recalled and rewritten. Textbook publishers however, experienced a corresponding gain in profits even though their products now contained as much creative writing as scientific prose. People graduating in physics and other hard sciences began wondering what exactly they had purchased with their student loans. Everything they had painstakingly studied and regurgitated on exams was now in question. A related statistic showed that for the first time in years, the hard sciences experienced a spike in admissions as young people everywhere saw an opportunity for themselves to play a realistic role in uncovering the world around us. As one graduating high school senior put it, "All the good stuff was discovered so it wasn't worth it, but now, there's good shit I could become famous for discovering."

My personal opinion was that the real reason for the rush was because the final of any subject with so few facts would be very easy to ace. It doesn't take a rocket scientist to figure out that that leaves more time to party.

*   *   *   *   *

As the sciences struggled, their more spiritual neighbors giggled with delight. While scientists are cursed with the need to "know", religionists are blessed with the ability to "believe". The lack of measurable data or concrete facts wasn't even a speed bump on the way to the sermon.

Almost immediately, the Bible and other religious writings were being reinterpreted, illuminating previously "misinterpreted" verses and passages, making everything clear for the true believers. Depending on who you spoke with, The Portal was the door to heaven or the door to hell, a precursor of the rapture or a punishment for the "homosexual, liberal, baby killers." To some it became a sacred shrine, to others the focal point of our modern day Sodom and Gomorra.

Church attendance boomed and unshaven men toting signs provided the public service of letting us know that the end of the world was near.

*   *   *   *   *

It, of course, was not. Unless you are not reading this.

*   *   *   *   *

The real tragedy was that to the mutual disappointment of both the scientists and the religionists, after the initial excitement of its arrival, The Portal did nothing.

Despite optimistic and pessimistic pronouncements and predictions, despite being the most watched, monitored, measured, protected, analyzed, sermonized, prayed for and talked about spot on Earth – The Portal never changed. No more have popped up. And it has never provided anymore clues to its origin, essence or purpose.

This doesn't make anyone happy.

*   *   *   *   *

"In an infinite and absolute random world, every possibility is a certainty.'

"That is a quote from Forbes Maxwell from the Book of Chance of 'ROAR -The Religion of Absolute Randomness.' You are probably wondering what ROAR has to say about the famous Portal. What does ROAR tell us about its meaning? The answer is simple. The Portal challenges scientists to discover its secrets. It challenges other religions to explain its purpose. But the fact of the matter is that The Portal does not challenge the Religion of Absolute Randomness at all. To the contrary, it's undeniable but unexplainable existence is an icon, perhaps THE icon, as to what ROAR represents.

"The one thing we can agree upon, whether we study the Old Testament, the New Testament, the Koran, nuclear physics, botany or beer

bottle labels, is that the Portal "is". For whatever cause or reason, it is among us. It is not just a possibility. It exists.

"Forbes' words seemed to foretell this moment. Its existence is a testament that we live in an infinite and random world."

*   *   *   *   *

If you look closely you will notice that the preceding four paragraphs are in quotes. That was a portion of a speech that Karen had written for me at the time. I remember it well because she was angry because I added the beer label bit. I must have given one hundred variations of this speech in the months after The Portal came into the national vocabulary. What was brilliant about it though, was that Karen had already started the machinery moving that would provide yet another wave of momentum in the ROAR movement.

She had already copyrighted the phrase "The Portal" as well as registered the "Portal Icon" to herself. She then created a contract between herself and ROAR allowing the organization exclusive rights to both for an additional percentage of the take.

Every staff member now had a business card that had a Portal Icon in the corner. There were billboards that had Portals so big that they had to add extra curved portions to the tops and bottoms to make them fit. There were Portal t-shirts, ball caps, jackets, coolers, coosies, key chains, car window stickies, decals, flying disks, water bottles, sun glasses and my personal favorite, urinal targets.

So now you know how we dealt with The Portal within the Religion of Absolute Randomness. Since it popped up after Forbes went down we had to be quick on our feet. It was simple really. It existed, so it was therefore possible and every possibility was a certainty. We didn't attempt to explain it at all, we just took the position that now that it was here, we expected it.

Now this is admittedly a little lame but, given the competition that was being presented by both the religious and scientific camps, it sounded pretty damn good at the time. So good in fact, that our already rolling movement, which had been the bastard child of an intelligent, if somewhat socially inept, deceased social worker and a marketing plan of epic proportions, continued to grow to become one of the largest organized religions in the last 1000 years.

And I was still Pope/CEO. Actually my role was more like the Queen of England, I primarily waved a lot.

*   *   *   *   *

I was also a "fornicator." At least to the Reverend Frank Fisher. Yes, the same Frank Fisher that was President Fisher and then Ex-President Fisher and the ex-husband of the woman who would have been my future wife. Who knows, maybe she still will be. There's still time to change my mind.

*   *   *   *   *

But not much. As I am writing this morning is hiding its stubborn little head just below the horizon so I'd better move on.

As I've previously mentioned, it is the night before my wedding and right now I'm sitting alone at my desk. Outside the wind is blowing. I can hear it blowing things around, mixing them up. It is one of the things keeping me awake. I wish it would just settle down and decide on a single speed and stay that way but every time I think its going to stop, it gusts up again. It's annoying.

I want it to settle down.

I want to settle down.

I want it to decide.

I want to decide.

*   *   *   *   *

Immediately upon learning of Marcus' most recent hospitalization, I made arrangements to fly to Key West. Actually, I made arrangements, Karen Eli Windslow undid my arrangements and made different arrangements. I then undid her arrangements and made more of my own. Either way, I eventually arrived in Key West and visited Marcus in the Crisis Unit.

As I expected, Marcus was not in much of a crisis. He was well fed, housed and outside of a rude nurse or two, he seemed well taken care of. I had seen him much worse off. His delusions seemed relatively under control and to my mind, he really didn't need to be there but he seemed to be taking some "time off" and was perfectly content where he was for the time being. He'd been around long enough to know what to say and do to extend his stay but still fall just short of getting him over medicated or beat up.

*　　*　　*　　*　　*

"… and then I woke up with a dick in my face and one thing led to another and here I am." Marcus finished his story.

" Are you OK?" I asked.

"I'm good. It was a good gig while it lasted but the scene was getting stale and it was time for me to roll anyway."

"Things are really rolling for me too." I said.

"I'm unconvinced."

"What do you mean?"

"Just what I said. I'm unconvinced that you really feel that things are really rolling for you. You're the freakin' Stanc driving New Age Jesus and you say things are 'really rolling'?"

We paused.

"I guess I feel your pain." I said finally.

"What pain?"

"You're right. I guess my scene is getting stale too. I'm beginning to feel like it's time to get out."

"Damn right my friend." Marcus said it with such certainty that it caught me by surprise.

"Why do you say that?"

"Cause your gravy train is as empty as the day after Thanksgiving."

"Gravy bowl."

"Whatever."

"What do you mean?

"ROAR is never gonna last is what I mean. The Portal's cool and all but when ROAR goes down, which it will, you're going to go down with it."

"How do you know ROAR is going down?" The ex-therapist in me recognized the red flag of defensiveness going up in my gut. I chose not to point out the fact that he had never read a newspaper and was locked in a psych unit so was hardly in a position to come to such a definite conclusion. As usual, he likely sensed it.

"I know I'm crazy. It doesn't make me happy. But it is what it is I think."

"I'm sorry…"

Marcus cut me off. "Just listen. I know you got smarter people than me telling you what's going down. And God knows you've treated me better than most anyone I can remember but even you think I'm crazy. And I could be wrong but what's in my head is all I know. I am good at running from the CIA. If I didn't have them, what would I do?"

"Yeah?"

"The point is that ROAR explains everything to everyone but doesn't give anyone anything. Folks – not just me - need their delusions." He got up to leave. "ROAR's going down."

"Wait." I said. "ROAR makes sense. That's what people want. Sense. Something more solid than a myth or a folktale."

Marcus smiled and shook his head.

"Listen," he said, "ever hear of crop circles?"

"Yeah."

"They started in England. For years people believed in them and scientists are saying that there was no way to explain how they could be so perfect and made so fast. Years and years they kept popping up in fields all over. I saw a special on TV when I was a kid about them. They said they was caused by UFOs, signals to space. Maybe some kind of signpost pointin' out directions or something."

"So what does that have to do with ROAR?"

"Damn! Just listen. A couple years ago these guys come out and admit that they were the ones who had been doing it all along. They did it with a stick with some rope tied on the ends. They'd just hold onto the rope and step on the stick, pushin' the crops down making circles and crazy designs. They started when they were kids and just kept doin' it and doin' it for years and years. They even took a TV crew out into a field and showed them how they'd done it. They did it. No doubt about it.

"OK, so?"

"People still believe they were done by UFO's." He paused. "Facts don't mean shit. People want to believe. You want ROAR to stick around? Give the people something to believe. Either that... or get out while the gettin's good. Look at you, you really don't want to be there anyway"

* * * * *

Here's another concern about my upcoming marriage… like a good ex-wife, my future wife has invited her ex-husband, the good Reverend, Ex-President Frank Fisher to our wedding.

This is of particular concern because the good Reverend has made a cottage industry out of crapping on me and anything associated with ROAR. Your first thought no doubt is, if he hates you so much why would he even bother to come to your wedding? But I believe he will come. My hope is that he will believe that he can seize the opportunity to show the world what a wonderful, understanding person he is. My fear is that he'll seize the opportunity for something less inspired.

* * * * *

After I saw Marcus in the hospital I began to worry about Norm. They had never tracked down the person who had shot him. After he recovered enough to go back to Golden Age, nothing much happened. He did move up a notch in the eyes of the WWXW morning show listeners. (Apparently, his part in the best selling documentary of all time had made no impression at all but taking a bullet and living, now *that* was something that appealed to the demographic.)

206

So I called my goon Wink Gates again. I had heard that after I fired him, Wink couldn't let go of his thing with Bo Bricker, finally cornering him in the restroom of a football game where Wink unsuccessfully tried to beat the crap out of him. It seems several exuberant fans walked in and, noticing Bricker was wearing a home team jersey, decided that Wink was a supporter of the visiting team. This was reason enough for them to fracture four ribs and blacken both Wink's eyes as Bricker slipped away.

I wanted someone to check up on Norm and to just ask around a bit to see if he could find out who at the Scientific Church of Light had decided to threaten Colleen. Because of the threat to Colleen, I had begun to question the idea that it was a random mugger who shot Norm. While the Scientific Church of Light was a prime suspect, I wasn't ruling out the Catholics, the Jews, Muslims, Native Americans, the Mafia or Microsoft for that matter. Bo Dick Bricker was another obvious choice and given Frank Fisher's new position as the grand reverend pooh-bah with the Fundamentalist Christian Alliance Church, he was also becoming a more and more reasonable alternative suspect.

Knowing Wink's history with Bricker though, I thought it'd be wiser if he focused on the Scientific Church of Light.

*   *   *   *   *

You may be wondering what was the difference between our new religion, the Religion of Absolute Randomness, and the other new, up and coming prospects like the Scientific Church of Light? First of all, at the risk of sounding like a homey, the Religion of Absolute Randomness is just a better name. The Scientific Church of Light is a hokey sounding oxymoron that sounds like someone came up with the name before the religion. But that's just my opinion.

However, I have noticed that where the Religion Of Absolute Randomness is "scientific" on the explanations but "light" on the rules, the Scientific Church of Light is "random" on the explanations but "absolute" on the rules. Go figure.

*   *   *   *   *

That said, and contrary to Marcus' dire predictions, ROAR continued its sprint up the growth curve. Profits were up. Karen the Agent was happy. Karen the Dog wagged her tail. Membership was at an all time high. We'd blown past the new age worship "circles" and were closing in fast on the old school churches. I'd been on TV more times than I could remember. We'd made the cover of *Time*. Karen Eli Windslow was trying her best to get me to look past Norm's "little shooting thing." And since no new threats had popped up, I was having a hard time disagreeing. Norm was getting more time than ever on the morning radio and seemed to be enjoying his pseudo celebrity status.

Marcus was out of the hospital and I'd set him up in a place in Daytona Beach.

And Colleen… we spent more and more time together.

*　　　*　　　*　　　*　　　*

"Thomas." Said the ex-president.

"Frank." I said in return.

"I'd prefer you call me 'Reverend Fisher'"

"And you call me Thomas?"

"I am older than you."

"So Colleen tells me." I reply with a smile.

Never happened. But if the Reverend Frank Fisher and I ever met alone, face to face, and if he insisted I call him "Reverend Fisher", that's what I'd say. Except in real life I'd never have the snappy come back in time.

*　　　*　　　*　　　*　　　*

Colleen rarely came to my "work."

After leaving both the White House and the former President, she had turned down the opportunity for alimony. A decision I would imagine that both pissed off and pleased her ex-husband. Pissed him off because even in divorce, his wife would not follow the traditional standards that stated that the man should care for the women and pleased him because he didn't have to pay her a dime.

While our forefathers took pains to ensure that our ex-Presidents and their spouses would be well cared for until their death, they never foresaw the possibility of an ex-First Lady. So while most former First Ladies spent their time doing public appearances or sitting on the Board of Directors of charities, Colleen had to work. Similar to her predecessors, she chose work with a charitable organization but unlike them, she was more than just a talking head. She was hired as an executive consultant for the International Coalition for the Homeless, a job she took very seriously and was very good at.

Colleen's job took up a great deal of her time whereas mine was... flexible. In fact, there were days when I simply had nothing to do.

On one of those days, Colleen happened to surprise me with a visit to my office with the intent of taking me to lunch. Both of us being pseudo-celebrities, sneaking out for a meal was a difficult task but ever since our first Big Mac together at the end of the White House tunnel, we both enjoyed the challenge and excitement of our elicit trips among the public at large. On this day, we had chosen to dress as tourists complete with cameras, sunglasses, black socks and sandals.

As we were about to make our way out the back door, Karen swept into my office. She tossed something on my desk and started to speak but stopped whatever she was saying.

"I wish you two wouldn't do this." She said waving a hand at our costumes.

"And I wish you were more like Karen the Dog." I said.

Unphased, she remembered why she was there. "Did you know about this?" She pointed to the magazine that she had tossed on my desk. It was a Scientific American Journal. The cover story was entitled "The Curves of Time."

"Time isn't infinite." She stated. "That's a problem for a religion based on a *infinite* universe and *absolute* randomness, don't you think?"

I honestly had never read a Scientific American Journal much less had any idea what was meant by the "curves of time" but I had to agree with Karen, it didn't sound promising. As Karen summarized the article, as relayed to her by her assistant, it became even more concerning. I was and am still not exactly certain as to the mathematics and physics of how time can "curve" but if time was not infinite but somehow could bend in upon itself and limit the randomness of the universe, it seemed likely that could damage ROAR. I understood why Karen was worried.

During Karen's discourse, Colleen had remained quiet but as a long but un-infinite silence descended upon the room, Colleen spoke up.

"I wouldn't worry about it much."

"If I was a former First Lady, I wouldn't worry about it much either." Karen said.

Colleen ignored her attitude.

"The universe is a big place." Colleen said. "As Forbes probably knew, the difference between very, very large numbers and infinity isn't that great. The fact that time may not be infinite doesn't necessarily mean that the principles in ROAR are inaccurate. While everything that has happened "must" not have happened the way it did, anything still "could" happen. I'm sure you could have one of your people check it out and write up some plausible sound bite that you could use should anyone ask about it."

Karen sat silently for a moment, then stood up and left the room.

"Is her universe big enough for me is the question?" Colleen smiled and asked me after she was gone.

"Marcus thinks she's a 'bitch.'" I said. "What do you think of Karen Eli Windslow?"

"She's a hard working woman."

I guess being a First Lady you learn to be diplomatic.

*   *   *   *   *

It's always what you don't see coming that drives you crazy.

A lot of things are clear from miles away. Another TV evangelist gets photographed with his pants around his ankles? Sad, but predictable enough. Another politician caught with his fingers in the back pocket of a CEO crony who just happened to receive more than his share of big time government contracts? Annoying, but practically inevitable.

Wink Gates giving up the private investigation business and becoming a front pew regular of the Scientific Church of Light? I never saw it coming.

Did I mention that Wink always wore a red and white Hawaiian shirt? He must have had twenty of them.

Wink started the second job I'd hired him for with his typical surveillance plan, which was to sit outside the Scientific Church of Light headquarters ala Magnum P.I., eat fast food, drink beer and make a list of everyone who entered or exited the building. I really don't know what Wink was expecting to

213

accomplish by this but to his credit, after a couple of days he decided he needed to change his tactics.

He decided to go inside, pretending to be interested in joining the organization and listen to their sales pitch. Wink reported back to me that he had given such a convincing performance to the initial interviewer that he had been invited back for "New Member Orientation". He then went back for the new member orientation and, as he later told me, "something clicked" in his mind and life was suddenly clear to him. He went to a few more meetings and the information he was providing to me began to slow, then trickle and then stopped all together. Shortly thereafter, he shut down his private investigator business and gave all of his money to the Scientific Church of Light and moved into the dormitories at their head quarters. He left a message on my answering machine explaining that he would not return the retainer I'd given him to find out who had shot Norm.

I have to admit that in a way, I was somewhat hurt that Wink let himself be brainwashed by a church other than mine. I know he wasn't that bright but the Scientific Church of Light is just... lame. Wink was however, able to give me enough information prior to his brain dipping baptism, to make me feel satisfied that the Scientific Church of Light was not behind what happened to Norm. Much like us, they were run like a business, but unlike us they were more of a corporation than a sole proprietorship. They had committees for everything and no decision could be made without floating it through the proper channels. Like committees everywhere, they took forever to actually do anything. Prior to bailing on me for the Scientific Church of Light's corporate version of Eden, Wink had been able to give me copies of meeting minutes from several of their top committees, including their taskforce specifically formulated to address the "problem of the Religion of Absolute Randomness."

They had only met once. The entire first meeting was an ice breaker activity.

*   *   *   *   *

Now that you know a little about the difference between ROAR and the Scientific Church of Light, I'll bet you're wondering how we dealt with our other big competitors? For example, how did the Religion of Absolute Randomness deal with the historical evidence of Christ? The same way the Christians dealt with the historical evidence of the Buddhists. And the same way the Buddhists dealt with the historical evidence of the Muslims. And the Muslims dealt with the historical evidence of the Wiccans. And the same way the Wiccans dealt with the historical evidence of the Hindus.

We ignored it.

Except then, after we ignored all the evidence, we went on to blitz the world with a marketing plan the would make a beer company proud.

*   *   *   *   *

I know what you are thinking. Or at least what you should be wondering.

So what about the threat to Colleen? According to the caller ID, it came from the Scientific Church of Light. How could they have been a threat if they couldn't get their own members past introducing themselves and sharing their most embarrassing moments?

For a while, we didn't know. However, while I lamely shrugged my shoulders at my ineffectiveness in doing anything about it, Colleen took action.

It seems that even a divorced ex-First Lady can make a call or two and secretive men in trench coats will start unofficially snooping around, tracing phone calls, tailing "objectives" and all the other fun things that secretive men in trench coats are supposed to do.

In his final days in the White House, President Fisher did not grow any closer to the White House staff. He'd lost the election and was about to lose his wife and he took it out on

216

anyone who had the gall to make a spelling mistake or miss a spot while dusting an end table. The Secret Service staff, who worked most closely and consistently with the President, seemed to take the brunt of his anger. Embarrassed by her soon to be ex-husband's behavior, Colleen often went out of her way to make sure that the staff received extra food or a Thank You card or at least left them with an apology and a kind word or two.

Now it was fairly easy for her to call up one or two of the ex-White House agents she had befriended and ask them to look into the threatening call she received. After talking to them, she found out that not only were they more than happy to help but protecting former First Ladies was actually within their job descriptions.

It was a fairly simple matter for them to obtain the phone records, find the number of origination and track down the location.

The call hadn't come from the Scientific Church of Light after all.

It had come from a large estate in Boca Raton, Florida. An estate with 10 bedrooms, two pools, two tennis courts and an outdoor shooting range complete with a bar built into a small, but upscale designer armory. You know how people like their martinis while they handle firearms.

It was no coincidence at all that the estate had recently been purchased by the ex-president, ex-husband, newly ordained

Preacher Frank Fisher. He had had a second line put into the house and registered it under the Scientific Church of Light. The phone records showed that he had made several other calls to Colleen, hanging up when the answering service kicked on. I wanted to know if there had been any calls made to 1-900 BUTT LICK or 1-900 TOE SUCK but it never seemed like the right time to ask.

So it was not a "random act of hatred" by a random member of the church in a world of absolute randomness after all.

Colleen later confronted Fisher about the call and he privately admitted to doing it but swore he really meant her no harm and that he still loved her and that he would do anything if she would only come back to him.

She didn't but the calls stopped. Neither of us really felt that Fisher would actually do anything to hurt Colleen.

*   *   *   *   *

And for Norm? They would later link the bullet embedded in his bible with a gun that was used in the robbery of a Stanc car dealership. He really was a victim of a random act of violence, like thousands of other people are every day.

*   *   *   *   *

While ROAR's continued success seemed to be pointing to the contrary, I was beginning to think that Marcus was right. Randomness did not always nestle neatly into the expectations of our minds. In a world where nothing happened that was not expected, we learned to accept to never expect the unexpected. Randomness it seems, on a very large scale, wasn't random at all but rather a very predictable set of events and circumstances.

Millions of gamblers play the slots and nearly all of them claim to win. Yet the casino creates a budget every year that estimates their millions in surplus revenue to within less than one percent. ROAR was exposing the house and in the process, taking away the dream of that one big pot that'll buy the condo in Boca or the boat or the facelift that they always wanted. Even great religious thinkers are gamblers. Pascal's Wager, for example, states that we have a choice to believe or not believe – to pick red or black – to hold 'em or fold 'em. According to Pascal we need to look at the pot odds when making our decision. If we bet on "believe" and we are right, we get eternal salvation. If we are wrong, and there is no pearly gated welcome wagon at the end of the tunnel? Well, we lost a lifetime of believing and were probably a better person for it anyway. The bottom line is in believing, the gains are high and the potential losses are minimal.

Now if you choose "not believe", according to Pascal, and you are right – you get to have a lifetime of wild orgy sex and debauchery if you choose but if you are wrong, you spend eternity burning in the fiery pits of a horrible cliché of a hell. The bottom line – in NOT believing the pay off is small and the potential losses are huge.

So according to Pascal, placing our bet should be easy.

If Pascal were alive today, he'd be wearing sunglasses, listening to headphones and making a bunch of money at the final table of the World Series of Poker.

ROAR however, didn't promise any payout. No sweet ring of quarters as they tingled into the cup of life's slot machine. No 40 virgins. No harps. No catching up with dead family members. Just the sterile, unromantic, useless, fascinating facts.

And soon people were going to start realizing it.

Or so I thought.

*　　　*　　　*　　　*　　　*

Karen Eli Windslow, again the agent not the dog, like Pascal, was also a gambler. The difference being that Karen tended to look at short term gains rather than long term gains. Each day Erik, Karen's personal assistant, hand delivered a volume of reports and opinion polls to her along with a grande cappuccino. And each day, she'd pat him on the ass and send him on his way and then sip her coffee and meticulously go over each number.

Although she never shared her thoughts about it with me or anyone else for that matter, Karen had predicted a fall months before I finally listened to Marcus and came to the conclusion that he was right. What Marcus and I didn't realize however, was that Karen was an extremely stubborn woman who did not give up on a metaphorical sugar daddy until she absolutely had to - meaning at exactly the point it ceased to be profitable. At this point in time, Karen was not ready to give up.

All she needed was a plan.

*   *   *   *   *

"It's gone."

"What's gone?" I asked.

I had just entered our new "Media room" for my weekly meeting with Karen and as usual, no "Good Mornings" or "How have you beens". Right down to business.

"The fucking thing disappeared."

"OK, I give up. What are you talking about?"

"Look." She pointed to the TV where Corey Cohn – yes, the same Corey Cohn who had broke the story after my forays into the White House – was gesturing animatedly about something.

"So, Corey finally made it to the little screen." I said. "I bet he married the producer's daughter."

"Sometimes your cluelessness is astounding." Karen said.

"In infinite, or near-infinite time," I replied. "there will be a world sometime, somewhere where your chosen messenger is brilliant and handsome but for now, you're stuck with me."

She didn't smile. She did look right at me, took a deep breath and said "The fucking Portal has disappeared."

*   *   *   *   *

Now remember, no one could explain why The Portal showed up in the first place. Nor could anyone explain what it was. Nor could they explain its purpose or even if it had a purpose. Given this general lack of knowledge about The Portal you wouldn't think that its unexpected disappearance would be all that surprising. You'd have been wrong. With an amount of vigor equaled only by the coverage of when it appeared, the media attacked the disappearance story on all fronts. There were more microphones and cameras than people in the former alleyway. The flowers that had subsided over time to a colorful carpet surrounding The Portal had, upon its abrupt disappearance, returned to their mountainous form. The combination of the people, the broadcasting equipment and the bright red, yellow and blue flowers being blown about by the wind – all surrounding an empty space where The Portal had been, combined into a surrealistic abstraction that played like a moving Picasso painting across TV sets all over the world.

The Portal had become the trademark of the Religion of Absolute Randomness and its disappearance was something akin to McDonalds losing their arches or Nike misplacing its swoosh. So while the random disappearance of the objectification of the principle of ROAR was not totally unexpected, there was cause for concern.

Karen was not happy. She was already taking action however and had already shifted her strategy to take full advantage to the growing pack of media outside our front door.

*   *   *   *   *

Interestingly, the competition, both traditional and new age religions, which had so recently been bending over backwards to incorporate The Portal into their theology, were now writing it off as a sign from above that the Religion of Absolute Randomness was the devil's work. God had finally prevailed and banished the demon gateway back to the pits of Hell from which it had obviously come forth.

I would imagine that the disappearance of our icon was probably the single best moment in the Reverend Fisher's life since he left the White House. I remember sitting in front of the TV, surfing through the channels, trying to watch something other than special reports of the disappearance of the Portal. I came across a religious channel interviewing the Reverend. They were talking about the Portal and while I don't remember any of the specifics of what Fisher said, I do distinctly remember the smug smile on his face. I remember not being angry though. I was just sad.

And tired.

*   *   *   *   *

There is really very little left to tell you.

My wedding is scheduled for later today. ROAR is in a state of confusion. While our explanation for The Portal's disappearance is exactly the same as for its appearance, people don't seem to be buying it. Karen is attending to damage control and doing an admirable job of it but I can see behind her eyes for the first time, that she's worried.

Colleen has been wonderful but I'm not sure she realizes the extent of the charade I have been able to maintain over the world and over her. I don't deserve her.

The morning radio show decided to dump their little routine with Norm and they haven't seen him at the Hideaway in weeks. I called the nursing home and they said he was getting a sponge bath – something he had vehemently refused in the past - and would leave him a message to call me back. He hasn't.

Last weekend however, my friend Marcus provided yet another grain of sand on the ever growing pile of coincidences that have been drifting up as part of this story.

After Marcus was released from the inpatient facility in the Keys, he made his way north, spending some time in Miami. He knows the system well there, so I'm sure he knew where to get what he needed. He also has a couple of old friends there who are card carrying alcoholics. Marcus really isn't a drinker but more than once since I've known him, his trips to Miami have ended up in Detox. I really don't know if that is what happened on this particular trip but somehow Marcus got picked up again by the police and taken once again to the local psych unit.

Marcus apparently had decided to head north again, this time along the coast. I know this because he didn't get picked up in Miami, he got picked up a little north of there in Boca Raton, on the newly purchased estate owned by the one and only Reverend Fisher.

My friends in the Dade County Mental Health system who shared this story with me are fairly certain the Marcus did not know whose estate he was on. He had simply wanted to go swimming. They also informed me that the Reverend wasn't home at the time. Since the world never found out about Marcus' role in our forays into the White House, the local authorities took Marcus to the psych unit where he promptly said and did all the right things to get released.

As of yesterday, I still hadn't been able to locate him.

*   *   *   *   *

I am tired.

Here's the thing. Do I not want to ride this train anymore because I think it will crash? Or... do I not want to ride it because I'm tired of the trip?

I guess the obvious question leading to the answer of my current dilemma is ... would I be getting off the train if it were going to continue merrily along its track to world dominance?

I guess I would.

Sometimes it's just that easy.

*   *   *   *   *

It's full blown morning now and as I am writing this the sun is beginning to show through my window. Sometimes, when things are going to hell, the best course of action is to take action, even if it is random action. I am tired but I think I've made up my mind. Thank you for your silent council and patience through this night.

I have decided.

I will cowardly run away from the difficulties with which I have managed to become entangled and run toward the only thing that seems to make any sense.

My friend Forbes will not be there. Norm will not be there and it is looking very likely that Marcus will not be there either. But I think I will just the same.

I am not sure about my future as the Grand Pooba of ROAR but...I *will* get married today.

Epilogue

I didn't get married… but not for the reasons I thought I wouldn't.

Since we last spoke my brain baggage has been totally shaken and mishandled. I had felt like I had at least put one of two things in order only to then have all my belongings ripped out and all my plans once again tossed all over the floor.

I tried to get married. I really did. The events that led to the halting of my wedding had nothing to do with anything I did on that day, at least not directly.

Let me start from the beginning, from near where I previously left off. I'll finish with a stunning blue-red sunset at a picnic table next to the bay at Rum Point, Grand Cayman, which is where I am now.

*   *   *   *   *

Friendship is something that most major religions treat like a twelve year old at a family reunion. She's there and cute but she has to eat at a separate card table with the five year olds.

Even ROAR left the subject off the table. It's like puppies, everyone loves them, what else is there to say?

My friendship with Norm and Marcus remains one of my most valuable achievements. Even more so today. Without my friends, I would not be where I am today. I would however, be a great deal healthier. Norm's condition did not allow him to attend my wedding. Marcus however, did make an appearance.

*   *   *   *   *

Lets go back to my non-wedding day.

As the sun rose, I still had not slept. You graciously kept me company through the night, listening to my ranting without judgment, or at least without any I could hear. For that I thank you. Because of that I am here now, writing once again. You deserve an explanation.

How much of my dilemma that night was typical pre wedding jitters and how much was caused by the events that I have described to you so far? I'll never know I guess. I know that as my lifeboat bounced from the top of one random wave to the next, I realized that I finally understood what was going on. I certainly understood and appreciated the intricate and near infinite series of cause and effect events that resulted in the world that surrounded me. Forbes' view of the random world possessed the beauty and balance of a perfect mathematical equation.

However, I also came to understand that by dipping my oar into the water, even in the vastness of the ocean of time, I could cause a ripple. Maybe just a small ripple but a ripple is a wave none the less.

I decided to deeply dip my oar and get married.

*   *   *   *   *

The sun came up both relieved and nervous... or maybe that was me. When it came time however, it and I shook off our indecision, banished the few remaining clouds and for the sun's part, she bathed the garden in a glow of late afternoon sunshine. As guests filed in they were cooled by an uncommon summer breeze and were serenaded by birds who seemed equally appreciative of the sun. According to Gill, our photographer, we would have had the best wedding pictures ever. Gill did not have a last name. Even though we never received any pictures, I recently sent him his payment and when I made out the check, I just made it out simply to "Gill". I hope he can cash it.

Gill was in a manic frenzy, firing off picture after picture trying to capture the perfect light before it slipped away. As you might imagine, the wedding day guest list of a former First Lady was made up of many attractive and well dressed people. Women in hats stood by husbands with manicures and talked of horses and charities. They innately knew how to pose for the camera.

Of course we had a videographer as well. Her name was Erma. Erma's last name was Smith. She was 43 and had been married four times but had never strayed from or even hyphenated her maiden name. While the pictures of our abbreviated ceremony never even made it off the film on which they were created, the video did survive. Until yesterday. We'd watched it several times prior to then. It was unedited but even in its raw state it was apparent that Erma Smith knew how to handle a camera. I also sent her a check. I added a little bonus.

Yesterday, I took the boat out to the east side of the island and in between applying sunscreen and pulling in tarpon, I tossed the tape into the ocean. It no doubt dropped slowly off the continental shelf and eventually landed upon the sand 2000 feet below the sparkling surface. Or maybe we live in the world where a tarpon scooped it up and swallowed it on the way down and where someday I'll catch that tarpon and while I'm cleaning it, I'll find the tape again. And maybe technology will advance to where the millions of 1s and 0s that made up the digital data on the tape can be repaired, put back in the right order and I'll get to once again see the tape and have a special showing for my great grand children. You know it'll happen.

It hasn't yet however and I really hope it doesn't. The tape went into the ocean because I really don't want anyone to see it. You see, Erma Smith unintentionally taped evidence of what really happened that day and when I tossed it, I really felt that no one else needed to know.

*   *   *   *   *

Under the perfect sun, among perfect people, with a perfect wife-to-be, I was having the perfect wedding.

Until someone shot me.

Bang.

As I fell to the ground, I remember thinking that the blood on my jacket was ruining everything. People were yelling and moving about in an unfocused stroke of action. It really didn't hurt as much as you would imagine. My head laid comfortably in Colleen's lap. She was crying. This was the first time I had ever seen her cry and it scared me. In one of those moments where your mind strays down unexpected paths, I remember feeling bad and saying "I'm sorry." It just made her cry more. And then I passed out.

*   *   *   *   *   *

Someone had shot me in my right shoulder, above my shirt pocket so even if I had been carrying the pocket edition of the King James Bible as Norm had been when he was shot, it wouldn't have done me any good. Had I turned slightly to the left, the bullet would have tore through my heart.

An ambulance arrived in an amazingly short amount of time, the immediate bleeding was stopped and I was loaded up and with Colleen at my side, I was carted off leaving a church full of stunned guests. To their credit, many of them made it to the reception anyway, drank Champagne and enjoyed the buffet. Good for them. I heard they even did the chicken dance.

My ride in the ambulance was equally entertaining.

I regained conscience in the ambulance and it didn't take me long to realize that I was not the primary concern of the paramedics who were treating me. The two of them, a man and a woman, did their job with an exceedingly brilliant display of speed and skill but the looks on their faces were not the "been there, bandaged that" look I expected. They looked frightened. Which frightened Colleen. Which frightened me.

"Is he going to be alright?" Colleen asked.

"Yes, ma'am, he's going to be fine."

"Are you sure?"

"Yes ma'am, the bullet missed all major organs and blood vessels and wound is clean. The bleeding has already stopped." They immediately busied themselves with my IV.

I never did find out the names of the two paramedics. I didn't think to look at their name badges as I lay there, not bleeding, waiting to arrive at the hospital. But then, I never arrived at the hospital either.

* * * * *

I couldn't help but notice that the paramedics kept looking forward toward the front of the ambulance. And then at each other. And then at the front of the ambulance and so on. My head was clearing now and I could see that Colleen noticed it as well.

"What's going on?" I asked.

"You were shot and we are treating you. You are going to be OK." Came the quick response.

"Which hospital are you taking me to?"

Silence. A quick glance among the two of them.

"I said, where are you taking me?"

"Sir," the woman said in a whisper, "we are not sure."

"You aren't sure?"

"What the hell is going on?" Colleen jumped in.

Again in a whisper, "We are not driving the ambulance. We do not know the man that is. He's wearing a mask, has a gun and we are going where ever he is taking us."

*   *   *   *   *

Just so you don't worry, I want to pause a second and let you know that the paramedics were correct, I was going to be alright. My wound is healing nicely, leaving a small enough scar as to not call attention to itself but big enough to be impressive if I ever want to prove to someone that I was really shot. I'm hoping that it will make impressive small talk as Colleen and I get to know some of the other couples on the island.

The ones we've met so far are generally both older and richer than we are and we've found little in common other than the usual pleasantries exchanged on the way to our boats. Isn't it wonderful to live in paradise? To not pay taxes? Nice tan and so on. They are pleasant enough folks but no one I really want to show my scar to yet. I think they'd be more afraid than impressed.

There is one however, that has seen my scar, Dr. Lafayette Stanc. Yes, the same Stanc family as the maker of my former "Pope mobile" A great nephew I believe. While I have never asked him about his famous family, I get the impression that Lafayette Stanc does not have a lot of contact with his auto making brethren. I also get the impression that he doesn't have a lot of contact with anyone off the island and wants it to stay that way. Maybe someday, we'll share a Hurricane on Seven Mile Beach watching young tourists in bikinis walk by and he'll share his story. However until then, I'll just have to be satisfied with the knowledge that while this particular Stanc may or may not know anything about carburetors, he does know how to discretely remove a bullet.

Dr. Stanc doesn't practice anymore and most island regulars don't even know that he's a doctor. The only reason I know is by coincidence.

*   *   *   *   *

So let's go back and I'll finish the connection for you between my hijacked ambulance and a 350 pound Jimmy Buffet look-a-like former doctor grudgingly removing a bullet from my shoulder. Before I do however, I have to mention the fact that the sunset I am looking at right at this moment, is perhaps the most amazing I have ever seen. The waves reflect the clouds that are glowing like the inside of a jack-o-lantern. Given a choice among the near infinite number of parallel lives that a random world says I may have had the chance to be a part of today, I would chose this one.

*   *   *   *   *

Colleen squeezed my hand tighter as our ambulance ride twisted and turned through the city.

The male paramedic looked out the window and over at his partner. "We're going to the airport." He whispered.

"The airport?" Colleen asked. "If they put him on a plane, will he be OK?"

"We've given him some medication. He'll be fine for a while but he needs medical attention soon."

I was feeling my fear subside as my bloodstream reaped the benefits of the medication. There was more soreness than pain and the comic side of having been shot at my own wedding, by someone other than the father of the bride no less, was creeping into my brain, causing me to first smirk, then giggle and finally to curl into uncontrolled laughter. The paramedics didn't appear to see the humor, trying to hold me down and making sure that I didn't pull out my own IV. Colleen however, had to smile despite the circumstances.

"Shut the fuck up." The driver of the van yelled to the back.

The ambulance abruptly pulled over to the side of the road.

"Get out." The voice said. Colleen started to move. I was still giggling. "Not you," he said "You, the medics. Both of you. Out. Now."

"We can't leave the patient…"

"I said out!" A rifle barrel waved up and down from the front seat.

They didn't need any more convincing. The paramedics looked more than relieved to be on their way and quickly scrambled out the back of the ambulance. The second the door closed, the van spun out back onto the highway.

"I want to know what is going on." Colleen yelled to the driver.

"Everything's fine Colleen. No one is following us. Trust me." Said the driver. The tone had changed. The voice was familiar.

The driver turned towards us just enough so we could see him.

He was wearing a Nixon mask.

"Marcus?"

The fact that my friend and former roommate Marcus was driving the ambulance that was heading to the airport after I had been shot at my own wedding – was very, very funny to me.

*   *   *   *   *

Marcus had shot me.

He nearly killed me, which according to him, was of course, my fault. He had hijacked the ambulance. He then dropped Colleen and I off at the airport with two tickets to the Caymans. Only one other person knew of this plan. Marcus may have had the sniper experience to think he could pull it off but he didn't have the money so he turned to Karen Eli Windslow for the cash required for the flight.

A thought has occurred to me many times as I have walked the beach over the past few weeks. Karen could have easily pointed out the recklessness of Marcus' plan and perhaps even done something to stop him. However, not only did she not stop him *and* give him the money for airfare but, immediately after I arrived in Grand Cayman, I received a mysterious note informing me that I had been provided with a safety deposit box at a local bank in Georgetown. Upon visiting this bank, I opened the box and found two sets of fake names with ID's and complete sets of documents. I also found that there was an account in my new name that contained a great deal of money.

239

While the bank officials have remained as silent as only Cayman bankers can be, I have no doubt that Karen Eli Windslow is responsible for the IDs and the cash. I also have no doubt that she is relieved that I am OK but I am *absolutely* positive that, if I had accidentally died, Karen already had a plan for making me the next martyr of ROAR. Based on what I have read in the papers since my disappearance, I am also very confident that my continued disappearance is what is expected in return for the money given to me.

*   *   *   *   *

While Karen's recklessness concerned me, I certainly wasn't surprised by Marcus'. What was surprising though was, with the exception of his total lack of concern for my body, Marcus had developed an amazingly thorough plan. He had worn a mask to ensure no one saw him. He had worn gloves to ensure he left no fingerprints. The gun he used has since been destroyed but if for some reason it hadn't been and someone were to have done a trace on it, they would have found that was registered to our friend Reverend Frank Fisher. Apparently Marcus's troubles in Boca the weekend before my non-wedding were not as random as they appeared. Thinking that firing a gun in the vicinity of a former first lady of the United States would certainly bring the CIA and the FBI even more aggressively after him than normal, Marcus decided to try to throw them a curve. He had stolen the gun along with the ammunition from the shooting range on Fisher's estate.

Marcus didn't even know about the fact that the Secret Service was already aware of at least one threatening phone call from the former President to his ex-wife. If his plan had somehow gone south faster than Colleen and I eventually did, Fisher would have been toast. It was a perfect set up.

Except for one bloody little detail.

What Marcus failed to consider in his plan to whisk me away from all my troubles, was that he was putting me on a plane with a gunshot wound. I sat down very uncomfortably in row 24, seat A. Colleen was in row 24, seat C. And sitting between us, in seat B, looking almost equally uncomfortable as I, was the giant Dr. Lafayette Stanc, reluctant heir to an automobile fortune and an even more reluctant solution to my bleeding shoulder.

*   *   *   *   *

And he did a wonderful job. My shoulder has healed wonderfully. I'm sure there is quite an uproar about our disappearance and I'm equally as sure that it will end sooner than my ego would like.

Colleen has already taken a job as a teacher at the island school. I'm not ready to work yet. Even if I was, I'm not sure what I'd do.

Maybe I'll write a book.

The world will probably find us some day but for now, my bags, both metaphorical and physical are unpacked. Norm no longer remembers anyone's names and is not allowed off the property without supervision but he enjoys his sponge baths and we have made sure that his medical bills and stay at the home will be taken care of for the rest of his life. ROAR rolls on. Karen, the agent not the dog, once told me that she would look after Marcus if anything happened to me. I doubt she meant it then and I doubt she'll do it now. Marcus, on the other hand, has agreed to take care of Karen, the dog not the person, for me and I have no doubt he'll do a wonderful job of it. He is on the move and I have absolutely no doubt that neither the CIA, the FBI or any of the numerous other governmental agencies who are investigating my shooting and our disappearance, will ever catch Marcus. In my humble assessment, there is simply no one in the world more qualified to avoid them.

*   *   *   *   *

As for me?

The sun has gone down and I think I'll stay here for a while.

I wonder if my tomatoes will grow?